Cruel Lies

Ella Miles

LIES SERIES

Lies We Share: A Prologue

Vicious Lies
Desperate Lies
Fated Lies
Cruel Lies
Dangerous Lies
Endless Lies

PROLOGUE
LIESEL

How is it that everything that dramatically changes my life is written in a letter?

The first time it happened was in a letter from my father. That letter was ripped by Langston, so I only got half of the truth.

But this letter, I ripped myself. I destroyed one half and plan on giving Langston the other.

Why did I destroy half of this letter?

The contents scare the shit out of me.

It changes how I think of myself.

It changes who I am.

If true, it changes everything. I won't let my world change all because it was written in a stupid, threatening letter, but I have no way to verify the contents.

Except…

No.

Time will reveal the truth.

Meanwhile, I'm left to wonder if the world is the one lying to me…

LIESEL

I GAVE up my son without ever having laid eyes on him. I never held him. Never got to see how many of his features matched my own. Never got to smell his sweet head. Never breastfed him. Never changed his diaper. Never dressed him. Never counted his fingers and toes.

I never did any of the things most new moms get to do. Even moms who give their children up for adoption usually hold their child at least once before giving them away.

Not me.

I had an emergency C-section. I was unconscious when he was born, so I never got to hear his first cry. I never met him. I didn't get to name him or find out what his parents named him.

I thought I'd never meet him. That was the plan. When I gave up my son, I did it for him.

I was young and not ready to be a mother, but if keeping him was best for him, I would have figured it out.

I gave him up because of who his father was—the most dangerous man in the world. I had no idea how he would have reacted if he found out the truth. *Would he have tried to kill my son? Would he have tried to brainwash him and bring him under his thumb like he did Enzo? Would he have had to fight Enzo to become the new Mr. Black, ruler of the most notorious crime organization?*

No—I ensured that my son would never be harmed, would never grow up in this dangerous and cruel world like I did.

So I gave him up, ensured he had the best parents possible, that he was hidden, never to be found.

And then, Mr. Black was killed. I could find my son. Kai did find him. It was safe to know my son. To love him out in the open.

But I knew better. Mr. Black dying changed nothing. We are all too connected to money, crime, and power for our enemies not to come and find us. We are always in danger. Enzo, Kai, Siren, and Zeke think they can protect their children while still living in this world—they're wrong. They will never be safe. I did the responsible thing. I kept my son safe. I gave him up a second time.

I thought that was it—I'd never know my son, not even his name, the color of his eyes.

Giving him up the second time was immensely harder than the first. The world turned to shades of gray after I decided to remain out of his life. Nothing brought me happiness or even a tingling of joy. I didn't smile or laugh, and I knew I never would again.

And then, everything changed.

I realized I made a mistake.

I had to find my son for his own survival.

I searched and searched, but I couldn't find him, not with all the resources in the world.

Then, I met Waylon Brown. It seemed like a coincidence at first, but eventually I realized he had ulterior motives. He knew where my son was; he provided proof. But in return, I had to marry him.

I would have married him that day, gave him everything I owned, and kneeled in promise to be his servant forever if he gave me my son. I still don't know what Waylon's real reason for wanting to marry me was.

Did he just find me attractive and want a good-looking, intelligent woman on his side? Or did he want the treasure he thought I had the key to?

The treasure.

Father, what did you put in motion? Why couldn't you just burn your letter? Why ruin my life and every generation after because of a rumor of the greatest treasure to exist on earth and only a Dunn able to retrieve it?

"Liesel, did you hear me?" Langston asks as he sits next to me on the beach.

I've been staring off into space, thinking about everything I've lost over the years. Langston is included in that list. And yet somehow, my enemy, my best friend, and now my lover might be the man who can give me my son back.

"I heard you," I say, having no idea what to do with the information.

I have so many questions.

"The others? Do they know?" I ask, referring to Kai, Enzo, Siren, and Zeke. I asked them all for help at various times in my search for my son, but none of them had been able to help me. Were they just keeping Langston's secret?

"No, they think he's my biological son."

I nod and look down at my feet. I still haven't looked at the boy Langston claims is my son since he revealed it to me. I'm not ready to see if he has my eyes or hair coloring. I've seen him before, but not up close, not while I was looking to see if he resembled me.

"What's going on in your head?" Langston asks, trying to pry beneath the shield I've put up.

I shake my head, but then I finally speak. There is no use keeping my thoughts to myself. Not when we've shared so much.

"I just don't understand. I don't understand how you could have my son. I don't understand how Waylon said he knew where my child was if you had my son. I don't know who to believe."

"I don't know why Waylon said he knew where your son was, other than he was trying to manipulate you."

"He had proof."

"What kind of proof?"

I shake my head. "It doesn't matter what his proof was, what's yours?"

I look Langston in the eye, and my heart swells. He looks broken from my doubt, but he's lied too many times. We both have. Of course, I don't believe he has my son. *But then, why would he lie?* I could easily get a DNA test and prove him wrong.

Waylon had DNA proof. That's why I believed him. *Will I believe Langston until I have the same proof?*

"I'll tell you my story and get a DNA test if that will make you feel better, but spend one minute with him and you'll realize he's yours."

My heart catches. *How can he be so certain?*

"I met Phoenix when I was a teenager. We met at one of Enzo's father's bars. I don't remember much about that night, except that I was horny and lonely. She was alone and in need of company."

"I don't need to hear this," I say. I don't want to hear about the night they met, fucked, and then how she eventually became his wife.

He grabs my cheeks in his strong hands, holding me so fervently as he peers into my eyes. "Trust me, you do."

I close my eyes, keeping the tears at bay. He was off fucking whores in bars, while I was dealing with the trauma of carrying my rapist's child.

"I was lonely because you were gone. Sure, it had been years at that point since you and I were friends, but even when we were fighting, I felt close to you. But then you took off for Europe. You left. You were gone. That pain was the first intense pain I ever felt. It left a hole in my heart. A brokenness I didn't know I was capable of feeling."

"You seemed to get over it just fine by running off and marrying the first girl you laid eyes on."

"I never got over you. I'm still not over you."

Dammit, my eyes water so much that I can't hide it. His words aren't the truth. They are empty, meant to manipulate me.

"I got drunk that night. I fucked her in the filthy bathroom. And then I left."

I grab his wrists to pull them off my face, but I can't quite do it. I revel in the feeling of his warm hands on my skin—even if I get burned, I want to feel him. That's my problem when it comes to Langston; I have no self-preservation. He's always going to end up hurting me—that's why I should let him go.

"A year later, I found out I had a child."

"Rose?"

He nods. "I knew I'd be a terrible father. I'd most likely end up dead before my child turned eighteen, so all I initially offered was money. I thought it would be better if I stayed out of her life."

He initially gave up his child for the same reasons I did.

"But then Phoenix reached out for help. I made the mistake of agreeing to meet her and my daughter." His eyes water. "Once I laid eyes on Rose, I knew that I couldn't give her up again. I wasn't strong enough."

His words stab me in the chest. Once I lay eyes on my own child, I won't be able to give him up. I need to make sure it's the right thing before I look at him.

"So, I became part of her life. I wanted to spend as much time with her as I could. But Phoenix wanted more than just a father-figure. She wanted me—something I wasn't willing to give her."

"What changed?"

"Fate."

I frown.

"I brought Rose to a playground. She was playing with a young boy her age. When she ran over to where I was sitting on the bench, she was dragging the young boy behind her. He was smaller than her, even though they were the same age. He had dark hair and was too thin in ratty clothes. It was clear he wasn't taken care of as well as he should have been."

I gasp—my son was hungry. He wore ratty clothes. I tried so hard to ensure he didn't have the same life I did. He was adopted by a wealthy family, or so I thought. *What happened?*

"I wasn't going to do anything other than talk to the foster agency and ensure he was placed with a better family. Maybe pay for his food or clothes—"

"I put him up for adoption with a wealthy family; he shouldn't have been in the foster system."

"His adoptive parents had died the year before."

My eyes bulge. *My poor son. Is he fated to live my same broken life? How can fate be so cruel?*

Langston continues, "I was just going to help him out, since Rose had made a friend, something she didn't do often. I'd been coming around for two years at this point, and she never made any friends. So her caring about this boy was a big deal. But then I saw his eyes."

He stares into my own eyes. "I saw his eyes, and it was like I had found a missing piece of my soul. Eyes who hadn't peered at me in years were now looking back at me. Big, beautiful hazel eyes. Eyes that belonged to my best friend. Eyes I would know anywhere."

My eyes.

My son has my eyes.

The tear that I've been holding back finally falls, rolling gently down my cheek.

"I couldn't leave him. I considered reaching out to you, but then I knew that you had given him up for a reason. The choice was now mine, not yours. I talked to the foster agency. I could adopt him; the only problem was Phoenix."

I wipe my tears. "Why was Phoenix a problem?"

"Rose took an immediate liking to Atlas. I knew I couldn't separate them. And I only had partial custody of Rose at the time. I knew I needed her to agree to take Atlas into her life. To love him like a son. She was hesitant to bring another child into our life. Especially when our life was complicated. I was gone working with Enzo for a long time, while she was left behind with Rose. I would come back as often as I could, but it still meant that she had to do more than her fair share of the child-rearing."

He looks ashamed as he says his next words. His head hangs down, and his cheeks pinken. "I told her I'd do anything to make it happen. Atlas was my son, and I needed him and Rose to have the best life. Phoenix has her flaws, but she's a great mother. My kids needed a mother and a father. They needed love from a supportive family, something that you and I never had growing up. So I asked her what she needed to make this happen."

"And what did she ask of you?" My heart is beating a

million miles a minute even though I already know the answer.

"She asked for more of my time. For me to spend more time with her and the children."

I nod, imploring him to say the next words.

"And she asked that I marry her."

My heart flatlines. Phoenix has everything I've ever wanted—a child of her own that she can love, my child, and my killer. She has it all, while I have nothing. I've been dealt all the pain, while she's gotten all of the happiness. It's not fair.

"So, you did?"

He nods. "I married her. She knew what she was getting —a man who would never be faithful, who would never love her, but would protect her and our children with my life. For her, that was enough. To have me be hers for an eternity."

I close my eyes, taking it all in. Langston married Phoenix so that he could protect my child; I can't fault him for that. I can't fault him for protecting my child when I failed. I can't fault him at all, even if it all hurts like a thousand needles attacking my skin all at once.

"Thank you," I say, opening my eyes, more tears plunging down my warm cheek.

He stills, like I just slapped him. "What?"

"Thank you, Langston. For everything."

He cups my face in his hands again, wiping away my liquified pain, searching for the heartbreak that was there before. He won't find it. All he'll find is forgiveness and gratitude.

"I mean it. We've been through a lot you and I. We've failed each other so many times. Hurt each other. It stings that you know my child better than I do. That you got part of his life that I will never get. I'm jealous that you married a woman when I always thought deep down that if you ever did marry someone, it would be me.

"But above it all, I'm thankful. My son needed someone to love him. I thought I was protecting him by hiding him away, but you—you showed him love when I couldn't. You found him, protected him, loved him. You became his father when you had no responsibility to do so. He wasn't your blood. He was the lost child of a woman you hated. You didn't have to intervene. You definitely didn't have to become his father. And yet you did. I can never thank you enough for what you did."

"I hid your child. I took him instead of telling you I had him. And I married your cousin when I could have chosen you. Don't thank me for that."

I grab his hands and lift them to my lips, kissing them. "No, you loved my child and became his father. The rest is just messy detail. I'll never be able to repay you for what you did."

He scrunches his eyebrows and gruffs but doesn't argue. "Do you want to meet your son?"

I hear the children laughing just feet away from me. My heart pulls toward them. I want to meet my son. I want to meet Langston's daughter. More than anything in the world.

But I have to make sure it's for the best to meet them. I don't want to bring more enemies into their life. When I meet them, it has to be because it makes their lives better, not worse.

So I answer the only way I can, "No."

2

LANGSTON

My mouth falls open. Her hands slip through my fingers, and my eyes are blinking rapidly. She's joking, or she just said the word because she's used to telling me no.

"Liesel?"

She stands and starts to walk away from me—away from the kids.

"It's okay to be scared. I'll be there with you." I stand, hoping to lure her back. She lived with a man and agreed to marry him because he said he could help her find her son. Now that I told her exactly where he is, she's running. It doesn't make sense to me.

Maybe she's scared? I'm scared too. I'm scared that I'm going to let my feelings for this woman cloud my judgment and change all my plans.

Liesel stops. She doesn't turn her head, but I can hear her words clear as day.

"I'm not afraid. I would love to meet my son, more than anything in this world, but I won't until I know it's safe for him." Then she jogs away, leaving me standing alone, stunned.

Why is she worried about Atlas' life? What is she hiding?

"Don't touch it! It could hurt you," Atlas yells at Rose.

I turn and start walking over toward the kids, quietly observing so they don't notice I'm there.

Rose is bent down in front of what looks like a jellyfish, a small cast still on her arm.

"But it'll die if we don't get it back to the water," Rose says.

"Then, let it die. It's not worth getting stung," Atlas says, grabbing hold of the hem of her black T-shirt and trying to pull her back. It doesn't stop Rose; she bends down and touches the creature. Just like Atlas warned her, the creature stings her.

"Ouch," she pulls her little hand back.

I shake my head at my daughter. So brave that it will get her killed someday, while Atlas is so cautious that he never really lives.

"Let me help," I say, walking over to them.

Rose pouts.

Atlas grins, his face shining like the sun.

"I can do it," Rose says.

"I know, but there is nothing wrong with asking for help."

I squat down and look at the still jellyfish on the sand in front of us. I scoop my hands underneath its squishy body and then carry it over to the water before flinging it into the ocean, setting it free.

I don't know if it will survive or if it has sustained too much damage, but as I stare out at the ocean, I feel a ping of jealousy. Whatever the outcome, the jellyfish is free, unlike me, who is bound by too many lies to count.

"Why didn't it sting you, daddy?" Rose asks.

I turn back to my daughter and hold out my hands. "It did."

Atlas gasps. "Does it hurt?"

"Not as much as watching either of you get hurt does."

Atlas stares at my hand with concern. He doesn't like other people being hurt. He'd rather take on the pain himself.

"Come here," I say to him, holding my arms out.

He collapses into my side as I kneel down and wrap my arms around him. "When you hug me, you take all the pain away."

"Good, daddy. I don't like it when you're hurt."

I smile and watch as Rose approaches me more cautiously but eventually wraps her arms around me as well.

"Piggyback ride?" Rose asks.

"Climb on, you two."

She climbs on my back while Atlas rolls his eyes at her. I know he'd rather keep his feet on the ground, but he trusts me more than anyone else. So when I lift him up in the air and fling him around, he laughs and it's completely carefree.

I glance down the beach toward where Liesel took off. I have an undeniable urge to run after her, but my kids are more important. I have to keep them safe. Liesel will come around.

I carry the kids on my back toward the house, where Phoenix is sitting on the back deck, watching and waiting for us. She doesn't say anything as I set the kids down.

"I'm starving," Rose says as soon as her feet hit the deck.

I chuckle.

Phoenix shakes her head. "There is some fruit and string cheese in the fridge. Wash up first, and then you can eat it."

Rose runs inside with Atlas fast on her heels.

I can't help but smile watching them. They remind me of Liesel and me when we were their age. They seem to fit together even though they aren't biological brother and sister. They still share some blood, being cousins and all.

I look back at Phoenix, who is staring at me intensely. She's wearing her usual outfit of dark jeans and a black long-sleeved T-shirt, thick makeup, and red hair. She hates the beach and the ocean. She'd rather us live in a large city somewhere, but she stays because of me. This is what I need: to be near the ocean. I spend my entire life either here along the beaches of Miami, on a yacht, or basking in the sun on my private island near the Bahamas.

"Why do you put up with me? Why not divorce my ass and find another man who would actually love you?" I ask. It's brazen of me and reveals more about what happened between Liesel and me than I should be admitting, but I have to know why she stays. Maybe if I can understand her, I'll have an idea of how we can move forward.

It doesn't matter what I want. No matter what becomes of Phoenix and I, I can't marry Liesel. I can't love Liesel. Fucking her is all we get, even though it's not enough for either of us to survive on.

"I'm going to need a glass of wine if we are going to have this conversation." She moves to get up, but I grab her wrist, my body begging her to answer me.

She sighs, seeing the pain in my eyes.

"I'm not a good man, Phoenix. I haven't been loyal."

"I never asked you to be."

"I know, but you deserve a man who is."

Her hand touches my shoulder. "Falling in love means you don't get to choose how. You just fall. I know you'll never love me back, but I'd rather have the love of my life in my life than live with no love at all."

I release her wrist, and she walks into the house. My eyes squeeze shut as the wind picks up, hitting me forcefully in the face, as hard as the reality of my situation.

I'm married to a woman who loves me and deserves to be loved back—something I can never give her. A woman who is a wonderful mother to my children.

Yet my body yearns for a woman who hates me and will never love me. A woman I can never love in return. A woman who is the biological mother of one of my children but gave him up.

My life is a fucking disaster.

One of my own creating. If I had just left Liesel alone, I wouldn't be in this mess. I wouldn't be questioning everything. I would be focused on what's important—being a good father.

I hear a car pull up on the gravel drive, so I walk to the front deck, already knowing who it will be.

Enzo and Beckett are stepping out of the car when I walk up to the driveway. Enzo has a heavy scowl, while Beckett is smirking.

"Find Rowan?" I ask, crossing my arms as I lean against one of the poles on the deck.

"Yes, no thanks to you," Enzo says.

I look around into the back of the SUV; I don't see Rowan.

Beckett laughs. "We took him to Enzo's house to have a doctor look him over."

"You should put a bullet between his eyes, not fix his wounds, after what he did to Liesel and me."

"Oh, relax, dude, you're both made of stronger stuff than that. What you two went through was barely a scratch," Beckett says.

My brows pinch. "So that makes what you did okay? Hiring a man to kidnap and torture us?"

"We didn't hire him. He already works for us," Enzo says.

"Fire him or I quit," I say.

"That's not my decision," Enzo says.

I shake my head. "Then tell Kai to get her ass here. I thought you were my family, my brothers, but I was wrong. You are nothing but lying scum."

"Don't blame Kai, she may be in charge of the Black empire, but she didn't make this decision on her own. This was a group decision," Siren says as she walks from behind the car.

I didn't notice the second car pull up.

Siren—*she's really alive.*

My eyes water, and my heart swells, seeing her alive. I've missed her. She's the only person who truly understands me. Everyone else here I consider family, I'd die saving any one of them, but only Siren would I die twice for.

Until now.

"I already know about your betrayal. You faked your own death to hurt me. How could you?"

"How could you kill Liesel's fiancé? How could you kidnap and threaten to kill her?" Siren walks toward me and puts her hands on both of my cheeks. "You were out of control, Langston. Liesel came up with a plan to get back at you—I just went along with it."

I growl and jerk back, forcing her hands to fall from my face. "You don't get to talk to me, not after what you did. You betrayed me when you faked your injury and possible death. And as if that wasn't enough, you decided to risk our lives to manipulate Liesel and me? You're the devil."

Her face falls. I've never been like this to Siren. I expect her to fight back; instead, she gives me space.

That's when I spot Zeke behind her. He lifts his fist and slams it into my face. I knew it was coming. I deserve it.

"That was for forcing my wife to suck your cock. If you weren't a brother to me, I'd castrate you."

I don't fight back, and I don't tell him that Siren sucked my cock willingly to help me. He's the only person who has earned the right to hurt me. All these other bastards had no right.

Kai finally steps forward. "It was my decision to have Rowan kidnap and torture you. Don't blame any of them, blame me."

"I do. And now you can all get the fuck off my property." I turn to walk inside. "Oh, and Kai? I quit."

3

LIESEL

ATLAS IS MY SON.

All the fleeting glimpses I've gotten of him over the last few weeks fill my head as I walk up and down the beach, tormented by what I should do. His dark-colored locks, his laugh, his height.

Is it safe to meet him?

What about what Waylon said? That my son isn't safe. That if Waylon died, so would my son. Is Nolan going to carry on in Waylon's place? Someone else? Or was it all a threat to get what he wanted from me?

The sun begins to set, and I find myself walking back toward the house. I don't know if I should meet Atlas or not. I don't know if I'll be bringing more danger into his life once again, and I refuse to be selfish where he's concerned. I'm glad I now know for sure he's alive and in a loving family. I need to make sure that Atlas is really my son, though, that Langston isn't lying for some gain. And if Atlas is, in fact, my son, I need to warn Langston. He needs to know so he can protect him if he is in danger.

I run my hand through my hair, already knowing that

Atlas is my son—Langston wasn't lying. He took care of him when everyone else failed. I can hate Langston for a lot of things, but I'll never be able to repay him for what he's done.

As I walk in the dark, I hope that the children have gone to bed. I need another day before I face them, but I also need to talk to Langston. I need to figure out what we do next. And it's not like I have any money or resources to leave Miami.

I hear voices as I approach the house and find the whole crew—Enzo, Kai, Beckett, Siren, and Zeke—camped out on the back deck, talking amongst themselves.

I stop, my feet halted in the sand. I don't want to speak to any of them ever again for what they've put me through. They had me kidnapped and tortured. They helped conceal my child from me even if they didn't know. They failed to protect me when I was raped. They failed to be there every night when I searched for my son until I had no choice but to accept Waylon's help.

I want to run and hide—but I'm done hiding.

I climb the steps loudly, until every voice on the deck silences at my approach. When I reach the top, all eyes fall on me.

Siren is sitting on Zeke's lap as he plays possessively with her hair. Both are wearing a dark T-shirt and jeans. Kai sits next to Enzo—both of them holding a glass of wine. Kai is wearing a simple sundress, and Enzo is in jeans. Phoenix sits next to Kai in her usual long-sleeved clothing, even though the heat of summer is still suffocating us. And Beckett sits in a chair alone, like he isn't part of the group at all.

I feel Langston sitting across from all of them, but I don't look at him. I'm just thankful he isn't sitting next to Phoenix.

For a moment, the only sound is the gentle flow of electricity through the Edison lights that hang overhead.

My eyes shoot through the souls of every person here,

silently cursing them for the sins each of them has committed against me.

I consider my next move. *Should I walk past them all and go into the house, or sit out here and have it out with them?*

No more running. No more hiding.

I spot a seat next to Langston and take it. For once, I feel like it's us two against all of them—something that I haven't felt in a long time. Langston has always been part of them. He always takes their side. But when I feel his pinky brush against my outstretched hand, he's letting me know he's on my side. Whatever loyalty and guilt he has toward Phoenix, whatever brotherhood he feels toward Enzo and Zeke, whatever soulmate bond he has with Siren—none of it matters right now. We've both been betrayed by all of them.

"So, what happens now? You two go after the treasure together?" Kai asks.

I glare at her, and I feel an agreeing animalistic growl coming from Langston next to me. Both of us are still wearing the oversized flannel we got from the cabin we were hiding in.

"You don't get to know anything about our plans," I spit back.

"As the queen of an empire where hundreds of employees and families rely on me, I make it my duty to know."

Langston jumps in. "It doesn't concern you, not anymore. I quit. My enemies will no longer be concerned with going after you."

That gets me to turn and look at Langston in surprise. He quit. I look for the lie in his eyes, but I don't find it.

His frown lightens slightly when I look at him.

"You don't get to quit. None of us do," Enzo says.

We both snap our heads in his direction. "I quit. I used to be part of this family but was thrown out years ago. I was written out of this family. I was considered the villain. So yes, if Langston wants to quit, he can quit."

No one responds.

And then Kai smirks. "At least our plan worked. You two don't want to kill each other anymore; you want to kill us. I can live with that if it means you'll stop bickering."

Her eyes say she knows that we've done more than just stop bickering. We've fucked each other, and if circumstances were different, we'd keep fucking each other until we no longer want to fuck any person.

But I feel Phoenix's gaze.

I'm the devil. I fucked another woman's husband. I don't care about the reason they got married. I don't care that they have an open marriage. It was still a sin—one that I don't regret. I still hurt the woman who has been selflessly raising my son.

I close my eyes, unable to deal with my own shame. I rub my arms, trying to soothe myself as the cool night breeze rattles through the empty place in my chest where my heart once beat. The only heart I have is for that of my son. And I'm more conflicted about what to do about him than ever.

"Come on, it's late; let's leave the lovebirds alone," Kai says, not mincing her words even though she sits next to Phoenix.

Finally, I let my eyes drift to her. She's not looking at Kai; she's looking at me. If my chest cavity wasn't already empty, Phoenix would be burning a hole straight through it.

Kai stands up and grabs Enzo's hand, dragging him behind her.

"Let me know if you need any resources or men to help you," she says as she starts down the stairs of the deck.

"Finish this," Enzo hisses at Langston. He doesn't like anything risking his family or empire. But Langston doesn't like being bossed around, and it's clear that he's done following orders after what they did to us.

Beckett stands and follows his half-brother. He doesn't speak or give us any of his thoughts, but it's clear his loyalty lies with his blood family.

Siren climbs off Zeke's lap and motions for him to follow her. She gives me a slight smile before turning to Langston. "I'm not sorry. You needed this."

She looks back at Zeke, who is standing still as a statue near Langston. I don't know what he's doing, but it appears Langston does.

"Get it over with you big oaf," Langston says, rolling his eyes.

Zeke's fist flies in Langston's face, knocking him back on the couch he sits on.

Siren shakes her head like her husband is a ridiculous overbearing bastard.

"That was the last freebie I'll give you," Langston growls.

"Good, it will give me more reason to hit you harder next time," Zeke snarls.

I realize now as I look at Langston's face, that both sides of Langston's face are puffy. Even in the dark light, I can see the hint of purple forming just under the skin. This isn't the first time Zeke has hit him today.

It makes me giggle.

Langston shoots me an *I thought you were on my side* glare. That only makes me laugh harder.

Serves you right for getting his wife on her knees to suck your dick, I shoot back.

You're one to talk. Langston looks to Phoenix, and my smile wavers. I've committed the same sin. If I was a better woman, I'd let Phoenix take a swing at me too.

Zeke and Siren leave. And then it's just us and Phoenix.

There's a heaviness in the air between us, threatening to

choke me if someone doesn't talk soon. I'm sure Phoenix knows what happened between Langston and me. Either because he told her or she's smart enough to figure it out. I just don't know what she's going to do about it.

I don't know what Langston is going to do about it.

I don't know what I'm going to do about it.

Phoenix yawns and then stands. "I'm going to bed. You coming, Langston?"

"Not yet," he says, meeting her gaze.

Not yet—those words hurt us both. Phoenix because he isn't following after her. And me because his words insinuate that he will eventually.

Her jaw ticks in disapproval, but she doesn't tell him off. I don't understand all the ins and outs of their marriage, but if she's married to Langston, she must know that she can't control him. He's a wild killer, and as much as he says he quit working for Kai—he's loyal to a fault. He'll be back to taking orders in no time.

"She can sleep in the guest bedroom in the basement," Phoenix says, not addressing me even though I'm sitting right next to Langston.

I want to snap back that Langston is hers. Even though I fucked him, there is no way he'll leave her. Not when it's the only way to keep both of his children together. Even if I am one of their biological mothers, it doesn't matter. Even if I meet Atlas, it doesn't mean he's mine. I haven't been in his life in years. I haven't proven worthy of being a mother. I will never prove worthy. She'll always win.

I don't say any of that, though. I just watch silently as she walks inside the beach house.

I don't think about how she has two houses, while I have none. I can no longer afford my apartment in New York now that Langston stole everything from me. And I no longer care about reclaiming what was stolen. I have one mission, one goal—to protect my son.

I suspect Langston's reason for going after the treasure is the same as mine. For once, we are on the same side.

"We should talk," Langston says once the night air settles and the surge of our electricity resumes between us. I try to forget about how good it feels to kiss him, to have him plunging inside me.

We have a lot to talk about, but all my body wants to do is feel the thrill of Langston exploring my body.

"We should," I say, not being the one to start the conversation. If I start talking, I'll end up kissing him, and now that we are once again safe, I refuse to become the mistress.

His hand twitches against the fabric of the couch we are both sitting on. Moments ago we were united against our common enemies—friends who betrayed us. Now I don't know what we are. In the very least, we're sinners who stepped into a fire about to consume us both.

"We should go to Peru. We should find the treasure. Then we can decide what to do—use it or destroy it. We have to stop our enemies from attacking us; there is too much at stake," he says.

He means Atlas and Rose. We can't have people coming to attack us for a treasure that we don't even have. We have to put a stop to it.

"I agree."

"Good, I'll see if Beckett wants to watch the kids. He's surprisingly good at it."

"You trust him after what he did?"

"He's the only one I trust. He didn't plan to have us kidnapped. He just went along with it."

I nod. It's not really my place to question the safety of my child, not when I haven't been in my child's life since he was born.

"And then I will book a flight for the three of us," he continues.

"The three of us?"

Langston swallows hard, like he doesn't want to have to state the obvious, but I'm not going to make this easy on him. "Phoenix has to come."

"Why?"

"Because the letter says only a Dunn who is married can seek the treasure. Last I checked, you aren't married."

"No thanks to you."

His eyebrows pull together, and his body tenses. "Actually, thanks to me. You shouldn't be married to a man who used your lost son to blackmail you."

"Ha, you're one to talk since you married Phoenix for basically the exact same reason."

He growls. "So I guess we are doing this? Let's have it. Yell at me for marrying a woman who has been raising your child as if he were her own son. Do it. Tell me how much of a monster I am for fucking you while married. I'm fucking horrible—I know. But I don't care about what you think of me or even what Phoenix thinks of me—the only people I care about are Rose and Atlas. They are safe and loved— that's all that matters."

Silence.

Tears water my eyes, but I don't speak. I can't be mad at him for marrying Phoenix. Even if he wasn't married, it wouldn't change anything. I still couldn't marry him. He'd never be mine...

Phoenix has to come. Even though she hates me. Even though I hate her. Even though I want to thank her and kiss her for everything she's done for my son. I still hate her, but I also owe her my life.

"Fine, Phoenix comes."

Langston settles back, surprised by how easily he won that fight.

"When do you want to leave?" he asks with a soft, bewildered expression.

"Tomorrow. I want everything done as soon as possible."

"Okay, tomorrow it is then."

Silence stretches again, allowing the sultry tingling to reemerge between us. The spark that we stoked, instead of extinguished, is a full-blown fire between us. We have to find a way to put it out, though. If we don't, it will spread until we've burned everyone we love in the process.

"You should meet Atlas before we leave," Langston says.

I shake my head. "I can't."

"Why?"

Waylon—that's why. Waylon still has a hold on me, even in death. He owns my soul, and I'm not sure if it's safe to see Atlas.

"I just can't." I look down at my hands, picking at my nails nervously.

I hear Langston move against the scratchy fabric as he slides toward me. From the corner of my eye, I see his hands grab onto mine, gently stopping me from anxiously twisting them around.

"You should meet him. It can be brief, and you shouldn't tell him who you are, but I think you should meet him. Just look at him so you can know he's your son."

"I believe you. There is no reason for you to lie to me." I hesitate a second, then ask my next question. "Do you love Atlas as a son?"

"Yes," he says without hesitation.

That's the only confirmation I needed to hear.

"But you won't meet with him?"

"No."

"Why? If something happens to us, he deserves to have met you. Do it for him if not for yourself."

I look up and pull my hands free, staring at Langton's dark eyes, avoiding his lush lips and sharp jaw I want to run my tongue over.

"No," I say definitively.

Langston shakes his head in frustration. His scowl tells me he thinks less of me for not seeing my son, not giving him the chance to meet his birth mother.

He doesn't know that I'm doing it to protect him. Even though Waylon is gone, someone will continue his plans. I don't know who it is, or if they will, in fact, continue Waylon's plans, but until I know for sure, I can't risk it.

For now, knowing his name, Atlas, and knowing that he's safe in Langston's protection is enough. It's more than enough after Waylon led me to believe that he was with a cruel monster who was abusing him. Langston may be a monster, but I've seen how he loves his kids. Atlas is accepted as his child just as much as Rose. He'll protect both of them with his life.

"I'll show you to your room in the basement," Langston says.

"No, I'd rather sleep here."

"Huntress, get your ass inside, now."

I look at the house. I can't sleep under the same roof as Phoenix, and I can't chance that Atlas might see me. I'll sleep out here under the stars, where the sun will ensure I wake up before anyone in the house does.

"Fine," Langston huffs off while I curl up on the couch.

I close my eyes and am just on the edge of sleep, when I see a shadow walking toward me. I'm too tired to open my eyes, but the shadow means me no harm.

A blanket is draped over me, and then his soft lips whisper near my ear. "I don't know if you are the biggest sinner or saint, but either way, you're mine, huntress. Mine."

4

LANGSTON

I BANG the coffee cup down on the counter and slam the cabinet door shut. I should move more quietly so I don't wake everyone up, but I can't. I didn't sleep at all last night. Instead, I spent the night in my office on my laptop, trying to figure out what Liesel is hiding from me.

I pour myself some coffee, and I stare out at the back deck where Liesel is still sound asleep on the couch.

What do I do with you, huntress? What are you hunting now? You've found your child, now what? Do you really want the treasure, or is that just an illusion?

"Morning, baby. What can I make you for breakfast?" Phoenix asks as she twirls into the kitchen.

I narrow my eyes, trying to figure out why she's so happy.

"I'm fucking exhausted and don't have time for games, so tell me what the hell is going on."

Her smile doesn't falter. She grabs a coffee cup behind my left shoulder and then grabs the pot behind me. She happily pours herself a cup before standing on her tiptoes and kissing me blatantly on the lips.

My eyes cut outside, but Liesel is still asleep. I don't have to ask any more questions to know what game Phoenix is playing at. She's trying to let Liesel know that she has me—that I slept in her house, that she's birthed my child and taken care of Liesel's, that she has a secure place in my life, while Liesel has nothing.

I shake my head at her antics. "Liesel being here changes nothing between us."

She tilts her head with an even brighter smile. "I know."

That's what she wants—nothing to change.

I sigh. What a mess I'm in. Two women who both are worthy of the world and I won't be able to give either of them what they deserve. All I do is take from both of them. With Phoenix, I take advantage of her kindness in caring for my children, but I don't want her body or love for myself. With Liesel, I take her body, her lust, her desire, but I don't want to love her.

"Beckett will be here in an hour to take the kids," I say, not giving Phoenix a say in the matter.

She nods. "And then we'll leave after that?"

"Yes."

"Where to?"

I take a sip of my coffee. Finding the treasure is between Liesel and me. Phoenix is only coming along because the first clue said that a Dunn had to be married to seek the treasure. That doesn't mean I'll share anything with Phoenix that she doesn't absolutely need to know.

"You'll know when we get there," I say.

Her smile drops, and her face turns dark. I think she's going to fight me on it, but there is a more pressing issue that we need to discuss.

"When this is all over, what would it take for you to agree to a divorce?"

She blinks rapidly and steps back out of my personal

bubble. She swallows and plasters a smile back on her face quickly, acting like I didn't just wound her.

I hate hurting the mother of my children, but I have to be honest with her. I don't want to divorce her so I can be with Liesel, but I'm not sure our arrangement makes sense anymore. I don't want our kids growing up thinking that we are in love, thinking our relationship is what a marriage is supposed to be. I'll never have Liesel, but I don't want to keep leading Phoenix on, giving her hope that someday I'll fall for her. I'll never fall for anyone.

"More than you're willing to give," Phoenix says.

"Money? I'll give you everything I own. Everything that the kids don't need to survive."

She shakes her head.

I set my cup of coffee down and encroach on her space. She's used to me manhandling her, trying to control the situation. I take her cup from her hand and set it on the counter behind her. Then I take her hands in mine. I need her to hear my words. I need her to understand that she's never going to get what she wants from me.

"I'm not a good man, Dunn." She winces when I call her Dunn. She prefers I use my last name as hers, but that's exactly why I call her Dunn. Even though we're married, she's not really mine. Using her maiden name reminds us both of our relationship.

"I take everything and give nothing back. I kill without a thought to the sanctity of life. And I'll never love you, Dunn. All I'll end up doing is ruining you."

She swallows hard, like she might be having doubts about what she's doing with me. "Then ruin me."

Her lips crash onto mine in a desperate attempt to remind me of how good we are together in bed. She's good because she lets me have my way with her. She lets me have control. But after finally having Liesel, there is nothing that will get my dick hard again except her. Fucking Liesel was everything I thought I could never have, and I won't go back.

I pull away gently, trying not to hurt her, but needing to make it clear that I won't be kissing her, fucking her, touching her again.

My eyes flick to the door, already knowing what I'm going to find.

Liesel.

Her eyes are dark, watery, and filled with pain.

Dammit.

Phoenix smirks.

I run my hand through my hair and step back. *Jesus, I'm going to destroy them both.*

Liesel opens the sliding glass door.

My heart pounds.

Phoenix turns with an angry glare, telling Liesel she's not welcome in her house.

Liesel doesn't look at me as she walks into the house, risking Atlas or Rose coming down and her being forced to meet them. All of her attention is on Phoenix, as if I'm not even in the room.

She walks over to us like she's on a mission, full of determination. Whatever she is feeling, it's intense and filling her entire body.

She stops and finally glances at me, but only to indicate for me to move the fuck out of her way.

I do, but I'm afraid she's going to slap Phoenix, so I stay close. Phoenix may have been playing with Liesel's emotions, but she doesn't deserve to be slapped.

I hold my breath as Liesel faces Phoenix. The two women who have twisted their way into my life deeper than I've ever allowed anyone face off. I should stop it, but maybe if they fight and get it out of their systems, they will be able to work together.

Liesel takes another step closer toward Phoenix, who tries to slink back against the counter. Then Liesel wraps her arms around Phoenix.

"Thank you," she whispers through wet eyes.

Phoenix exhales and wraps her arms around her. "You're welcome."

The two hold each other like they are long lost friends. I was wrong. They won't fight over me or stake a claim. They are better than that. All they care about is their shared love for their children.

It's a beautiful moment—one that doesn't happen too often in my life.

Liesel steps back, letting go of Phoenix. "I'm sorry."

"What for?" Phoenix asks.

I think Liesel is going to say for not being there for her child, for forcing her to have to take care of her child. She doesn't mention Atlas, though. "He's yours. I'm sorry for hurting you. I'm sorry for trying to take him from you. I won't again."

I won't again.

Those words are meant for me as much as they are meant for Phoenix.

Liesel won't kiss me again, touch me again, fuck me again. That's what her words mean.

My heart seizes. I thought it would be my cock or lips that was disappointed with her statement, not my fucking heart. It's like my heart can't take the prospect of not having even a chance of falling for Liesel.

I never had a chance of falling for her. I never would allow myself.

Mine isn't the only heart in the room that's breaking. I just can't tell if it's Phoenix's heart knowing what transpired between Liesel and me, or Liesel's knowing she can never be with me again.

"We need to get the kids somewhere safe and leave as soon as we can," Liesel says like she didn't just make a proclamation that destroyed us all.

"Beckett will be here within the hour," I say.

"We can't wait that long," she says, and then she pulls a letter from her pocket and hands it to me. "It was lying on top of me when I woke up this morning. Someone is here."

I grab the note and read.

Your child isn't safe. I can get to him. I can hurt him. There is nowhere you can hide him from me.

Soon, I'll come for the treasure. Give it to me or I'll take him from you forever.

The note is torn at the top, and I realize this isn't the full letter. I flip it front and back like the second half of the letter is going to suddenly appear to me.

"Where is the other half of the letter, huntress?" I ask, glaring at her.

She shakes her head.

"Dunn, go get the kids packed and ready to go. And bring Liesel a change of clothes."

Phoenix nods and runs off, but not before I see the hint of her smirk. Of course, she'd be happy that I'm about to get into a fight with Liesel.

"Give. Me. The. Other. Half. Of. The. Note."

"No."

"Why the hell not? We are on the same side! We both want to protect the kids. I can't help if I don't know what we are facing."

"I gave you the important part. The rest was for my eyes

only. It doesn't matter what it said. What matters is we figure out a way to keep the kids safe!"

She's fuming.

I'm fuming.

And when fire meets fire—an explosion happens.

An explosion won't help.

"What are you hiding, huntress?"

"What are you hiding, killer?"

I step toward her. She steps back, until the counter hits her ass, and there is nowhere for her to go.

"You won't again, huh?" I ask, encroaching on her personal space and taking up all the oxygen around her until I control when she breathes. My body hovers over her until a buzzing shoots between us, increasing her pulse.

She licks her lips.

I run mine over my teeth hungrily.

"I won't—I won't hurt her. Not after what she's done for me."

"What if I told you it didn't hurt her?"

"It does. She loves you."

She's probably right that Phoenix loves me, but it can't be true. Phoenix is too smart to have already fallen for my dumb ass.

"And if she were to stop caring about me? What then?" I breathe over her lips, tempting her to close the gap.

"Then…" she purrs but doesn't answer.

"How do you feel, huntress?" My thumb touches her swollen lip, begging her to give in to me. To want me. To let down her guard so I can figure her out. "What do you want?"

My tongue darts out of my mouth to taste hers.

She closes her eyes as my tongue brushes against her lip. They fly back open a second later.

"No." She puts her hand on my chest and pushes me hard. "You can tease me, tempt me, lust after me, but it's a waste of time. I don't regret what we did. I thought we were going to die in that tower. But things are different now. I won't hurt the mother of my child."

The mother of *her* child. The mother of *my* child.

I take a deep breath and sigh.

"Then I guess I'm the bigger monster between the two of us because I want to sin with you no matter who it hurts."

5

LIESEL

I'm stronger than I ever imagined. It took every bit of my strength to resist Langston. The wetness of his tongue against my lip, the heat from his breath, the pull of my soul. My body comes alive when I'm with Langston. I've never felt so alive as when he's inside me. And I'll never feel that alive again.

I meant what I said—*never again.*

I will take the memories with me forever, but that's all I'll take.

Langston's words will taunt me, though. They beg me to give in, and I'm sure his latest attempt was only the beginning. I can't be alone with him. I'm strong, but I'm not strong enough to keep saying no. Especially not now that I know how it feels to be with him.

I hear footsteps upstairs—Phoenix getting the kids ready. If I could make him fall in love with her, I would. It would be better for everyone.

All I can focus on now is the threat made against Atlas. My entire life has been about keeping him safe. It's the only

39

thing I've succeeded at, and I'll do everything I can to keep him safe.

Langston is desperate to know what the note said, but it's my burden to bear. It's my fault Atlas is in danger. And Langston knowing will just get him killed.

Monsters come in all shapes and sizes, but they all hide in the dark. Creeping through the shadows, pretending that they have the power to destroy, but that makes them easier to catch. This monster left a clue as to who he is. Now, all that's left to do is to decide if I want to set a trap and catch the monster or give in to his demands.

There's a rough knock on the door.

"Beckett got here early," Langston says, running to the door.

Thank god.

I hear footsteps coming down the stairs, and I creep back. This isn't how I'll meet my son, not like this.

I run out back before the kids make it down the stairs. I exhale sharply as the sun beats down on me, making me sweat. My hands are clammy, and my nerves shot. I need to run to get some energy out and make myself feel better, but I can't.

Instead, I do something that might actually help protect my kids. I call Siren.

"Hello?" Siren answers.

"Hey, it's Liesel. I need your help."

"I'm out of the faking my death business. Besides, I don't think Langston would fall for that one again."

"No, it's nothing like that. The kids..." I find I can't finish before tears fill my eyes.

"Say no more. What do you need us to do?"

"Make people believe that you all are moving precious cargo. Beckett will be the one who has them, but anything to make people believe that you or Kai or someone else might be hiding them, the safer they'll be."

I hate asking. They all have kids that this could be putting at risk as well.

"Done."

I exhale sharply after holding my breath, waiting for her answer.

"We all have kids. We know how terrifying it can be to be worried about your children. Don't worry about what was said or done before. When it comes to our kids, we will always protect them."

"He told you then?"

"That Atlas is your son? Yes. He told us, but I've always suspected."

"Thank you," I say before we hang up.

I hear voices and the opening of a car door. It's safe to go back into the house now and hide until they are gone. Saying goodbye as my son is driven away is not the way I should meet him. I haven't earned the right to meet him, not until I know he's safe from this world forever.

But I can't fight the pull. *Maybe I'm not as strong as I think? Or maybe I just love my son more than I care about Langston?*

I walk up the side of the house, following the sound of the sweet little voices. One is thrilled about the new adventure she's going on. The other concerned and dubious of why the adventure is being sprung on them.

I force my feet to stop when I get to the side of the house, where a row of bushes gives me a spot to hide. I crouch down, blending with the greenery.

And then I look through the branches and leaves.

I see a scrawny fair-haired girl in a pink dinosaur shirt, black shorts, and sparkly shoes. She has a black bandana in her hair, and she's talking Langston's head off about how he has to promise he'll be coming with on the next adventure.

He promises.

I smile. She has him so wrapped around her little finger. He gives her a tight hug, and I see how clearly her hair color matches his. She didn't get her coloring from her mother unless Phoenix's darker hair is dyed that way. She moves to hug Phoenix next while Langston moves to Atlas.

His hair is much darker, and he's more reserved. He doesn't say much. I find myself afraid that Langston is going to behave differently toward him since he's not his biological son, but he kneels down in front of him in the same way he did to Rose.

"Keep Rose out of trouble for me, okay?"

"I promise."

He wraps Atlas in a hug and then whispers something into his ear that makes him smile.

I gasp when I see Atlas' eyes and smile. There is no doubt in my mind that he's my son and that Langston loves him as his own. My only role in my child's life is to ensure that he's safe. I don't get to know him—that will only bring more danger into his life.

Phoenix is his mother.

Langston is his father.

And I, I'm his protector.

6

LANGSTON

I PLANT my feet firmly on the ground on my driveway as I watch Beckett drive away with my kids in the backseat. Every instinct in my body tells me to run after them. I'm their protector. I'm supposed to keep them safe. I need to be with them.

My feet don't move, though. The weight of the world is the only thing keeping me from running after Beckett's bulletproof SUV. The only way to protect them is to get the damn treasure and destroy our enemies. If they stay with me, they will be a target.

So I let them go, even though I physically feel pain letting them out of my sight. Even though I trust Beckett. Even though I know the rest of the Black empire—Enzo, Kai, Siren, and Zeke—will protect them. We would all lay down our lives to protect the kids.

I turn around just as the SUV turns a corner and escapes from sight.

Liesel.

She's standing on the side of the house.

43

I smile—she couldn't help herself. She took a peek at the kids.

I wish she had done more, met them, but that's her decision. The monster inside me isn't satisfied with that, though. I can forgive Liesel for a lot of things, but not when it comes to her child.

She looks back to the house and walks over to where Phoenix and I stand.

"We should go now," Liesel says. She rushes toward the car in the garage.

Phoenix and I exchange glances before we follow her to the car. I sit in the driver's seat, Phoenix next to me, and Liesel behind me. Phoenix tosses Liesel a change of clothes as I start driving us to the airport.

We aren't out of the garage for two seconds when a nearby explosion rocks our car.

Phoenix shrieks.

My heart stops.

Liesel just stares down the road, completely unfazed.

"It's gone," Phoenix says, drawing my attention away from Liesel and back to the house.

Flames dance across the shattered remains. This house is where my kids have grown up. It's where I first brought them home, where we became a family.

I try to push out the dozens of stuffed animals, bikes, and pictures that were just taken from us. We are all safe—that's what matters.

But my blood boils. Liesel isn't surprised at all that the house just exploded. *The letter threatened us, but did she hide details from me? What else is in that damn letter?*

I grip the steering wheel in rage and look back at Liesel through the rearview mirror. I've only been this pissed at her one time before. But this time, I'm not going to let her get away with it.

Phoenix is still sobbing and carrying on next to me. It's just a house, just stuff, but I feel her pain. Something was taken from us today, and whomever it was is going to pay—even if the woman in the back seat had something to do with it.

I reach across and find Phoenix's hand. I lift it to my lips and kiss the back of her hand.

"It's going to be okay, Phoenix. We are all safe. Everything inside is replaceable. And I'm going to make every person who had anything to do with this suffer."

Liesel's eyes meet mine when I say those words, intending her to know that whatever has happened between us doesn't matter. I don't care that we survived hell together. I don't care that she's Atlas' birth mother. If she had anything to do with this, if she hid this from me, then I'll make her pay.

I watch as her eyes drop to where my fingers are intertwined with Phoenix's. She doesn't react, at least not on the outside, but I suspect Liesel is raging with jealousy.

For the next few minutes, the only sounds that fill the car are Phoenix's quiet sobs and hiccups.

"We're being followed," Liesel says carefully.

I glance in the rearview mirror and force myself to look beyond Liesel to the road. A blacked out sedan creeps after us.

I make a last-minute right turn onto a side street, and sure enough, the car turns as well.

"Shit," I say.

"Oh my god! We are going to die. I should have gone with the kids. The kids are going to grow up without parents," Phoenix howls.

I let go of Phoenix's hand and grip the wheel. I don't have time to deal with her hysteria. I have to get the car behind us off our tail.

I make another sharp turn, and Phoenix screams at my sudden speed.

"Slow down!" she shouts.

I don't.

I take my gun out, preparing to shoot the tires of the trailing car behind me.

"Langston! Don't shoot them! I—"

Slap.

Liesel has unbuckled herself, climbed in between us, and slapped Phoenix in the face.

"Stop it. Now isn't the time to freak out. It's not helpful. If you want to be helpful, shut up and do whatever Langston tells you to do. If you do that, your kids will grow up with a loving mother and father. If you don't, then I'm going to throw you out of this car to ensure that your kids at least grow up with a father," Liesel says, getting into Phoenix's face.

I raise an eyebrow, not sure that's the best technique to get Phoenix to stop.

Phoenix sniffles then nods.

Then both women turn toward me.

"At the next intersection, I'm going to spin us. Then, I'll fire some shots out my window that will stop the car from pursuing us. I need you both to duck down. The car is bulletproof, but the windows are the most vulnerable."

Phoenix sucks in her snot and then ducks down, flinging her arms over her head.

"Seatbelt, then duck," I say slowly to Liesel.

Liesel rolls her eyes, then digs under my seat before coming back up with a gun in her hand.

"What are you doing?" I ask.

"Stepping up."

"You could get killed."

"Then I'll die doing something good for Atlas."

My heart swells. Maybe I was wrong about Liesel.

I give Liesel a look of preparation.

She grabs onto the door, and we both lower our windows.

And then I sling us around.

I aim out the window and start firing at the tires. I hit the first before moving to the second and seeing that it has already been blown out by Liesel. Then we both start shooting at the driver.

The men in the car barely get a return shot off before I'm spinning us back around and stepping on the gas.

"Is it over?" Phoenix says from the floor as Liesel and I roll up our windows.

I glance in the rearview mirror; the car behind us has stopped. I look to Liesel, who purses her lips and lets out a slow breath. She's always said she doesn't belong in this world and that she hates firing a gun. She hates the violence, but she fits in better than she will ever admit.

"Yes, the car isn't following us anymore," I reply.

"Good," Phoenix pants next to me. Her hair is disheveled, and her forehead is sweaty. Now I'm regretting bringing her along; that car chase is going to be the least dangerous thing we go through.

The rest of the drive is uneventful as I pull up to the tarmac where one of Kai's private jets is waiting.

"Huntress, go into the jet and tell them we'll be ready to take off in five minutes. I need to talk to Dunn here."

Liesel hesitates as she opens the door, but then she climbs out, still holding onto the gun like most women would a purse, completely at ease with herself. She's turned into a mama bear willing to do whatever it takes to protect her child—fucking finally.

Phoenix carefully watches Liesel climb the steps into the jet.

"We're on the same side," I say.

Phoenix pulls the visor down and starts blotting underneath her eyes, where her mascara has run. She pinches her cheeks and then runs her hand through her hair before she faces me with watering eyes.

"We're not."

"Yes, we are. Liesel cares about Atlas and Rose just as much as we do."

She shakes her head. "She hasn't been around. She gave Atlas up. She—"

"She didn't have a choice. Giving Atlas up was the best thing for him."

"I don't trust her."

"She's Atlas' mother. She knows Rose is my kid. Don't let your jealousy impede your thinking."

She slaps me.

"I'm not jealous of Liesel. You can stick your dick into anyone you want. The only people I care about are Atlas and Rose, and I don't trust your whore. She gave up Atlas, and Rose means nothing to her."

"You're wrong."

"I'm not willing to risk our kids' lives on your hunch, which is based entirely on wanting to fuck the woman."

"What do you want, Phoenix? We need Liesel in order to end this. The kids are safe. So you either trust her enough to finish this together, or you go hang out with the kids until this is over—which will it be?"

She huffs like the decision is going to be the death of her, and then she pops open the door. "I'm coming, but it doesn't mean I trust her yet."

"You don't have to trust her. You have to trust me." I grab onto her hip, pulling her back into the car. "Can you do that? Trust me?"

"I trust you."

I release her, and then we both get out of the car and walk up the stairs to the plane.

I don't spot Liesel initially when I step into the aisle. For a second, my heart skips, thinking that she took off. We need her help to get the treasure, to protect the kids.

I need her.

But then I spot her blonde locks peek up over the last seat in the back of the plane. There are a dozen seats between me and her. Phoenix takes the first seat at the front, purposefully making me choose between her and Liesel.

I sigh and take a seat next to Phoenix. I don't know how to fix the iciness between the two of them, but I'll let Liesel think she's safe for now hiding in the back of the plane. She's not safe—not from me.

7

LIESEL

THIS IS NEVER GOING to end.

Atlas will never be safe.

And it's all my fault.

The plane takes off with Phoenix and Langston sitting in the front while I occupy the last seat—the furthest away I can be from them. I quickly change out of my flannel and sweatpants and into new clothes—dark jeans and a tight white T-shirt. At least it's not a long-sleeved shirt like Phoenix usually wears.

I need to think, and Langston distracts me. My body comes alive when he's close, and if he touches me…forget it. There won't be any blood left in my brain to function.

I swore when I gave Atlas up that I was doing it to protect him. Everything I do is to protect him. I won't let anyone distract me.

The words of the letter burn into my head. There is only one way to protect Atlas now, and I'm not sure I'm strong enough to pull it off.

I close my eyes and lean my chair back so I can be well-rested when we get to Peru.

51

"What aren't you telling me, huntress?" Langston asks, jolting me awake.

My body heats, and my pulse races, even though my eyes remain closed.

"You can't ignore me, huntress. You are trapped on a private jet with me for another two hours. Talk to me, or I'll make you talk."

My eyes fly open, and I stare him down as he stands above me. I'm tired of his threats. His harsh words should tamper down the heat in my body, but the heat only rises. I prefer us being enemies to friends, even if we are enemies on the same side. It reminds me that I can never have Langston; he isn't mine.

"Your threats mean nothing to me."

"I know, but they should." He sinks into the chair next to me.

I think I prefer him towering over me to sitting so close. He leans over, invading my space as his hot breath dances across my skin on my neck.

"Won't Phoenix be missing you?"

"Phoenix is a big girl. She can sit on a plane for a few minutes all by herself."

I glance her way and see a thin black cord hanging down from her ear. She's listening to something, and her eyes are closed.

I sigh. There is no one to save me from Langston. Right now, I'd even take Phoenix's snarky comments—anything to not be left alone with Langston.

Langston turns sideways in his seat. He places one hand on the window behind me and his other hand on my chin.

"What aren't you telling me?" he asks again.

Everything. I'm not telling you everything because it's not your burden to bear. You've done enough. You've protected my son when he wasn't even your own blood. I'm the only one who can save him now.

"I've told you everything." *Everything that you need to know.*

"I don't believe you, Liesel. I know you're lying. You tore the note in half before you gave it to me. You knew the house was going to explode. What aren't you telling me?"

His grip under my chin strengthens as his resolve weakens. His voice is low and grumbly. He's trying to look strong and unbreakable, but there is a hint of the boy I used to know underneath his blonde eyelashes. He wants me to tell him not because he's worried about our safety but because I want to share information with him. Because I trust him. I do trust him more than he'll ever know. If I didn't trust him, I'd take Atlas far away from him. He's the only man I trust with my son.

I just can't let him further into the depths of my dark soul. I know what I have to do, and Langston will hate me for it. I can handle the hate if I didn't know anything else, but I can't handle him hating me after feeling his love.

"I'm not hiding anything from you, killer. I've told you everything you need to know to keep us safe."

"What was on the other half of the note?"

"Just a personal attack against me. Something about calling me a bitch and whore, I didn't think you needed to read it."

His eyes narrow, and his tongue licks his lips. "Liar."

Of course I'm lying, but I refuse to tell him the rest. Not until I know it's the truth myself. Not until I've done what needs to be done.

"So what if I am lying? You're not going to be able to get me to tell you the truth, so drop it."

"Kai and Siren are going to be disappointed their plan failed so quickly. Just like that, you don't trust me anymore."

"I never trusted you."

"I beg to disagree. You seem to trust me plenty with my cock in your mouth and tight cunt. Should I remind you?"

"You wouldn't do that to Phoenix." My chest rises and falls in hushed breaths.

Langston smirks. His eyes turn a wicked shade of black.

My mouth dries, just imagining his lips on mine. It's all I ever crave. If it wasn't for Atlas, my every thought would be consumed with Langston. I'd fuck him right here and not give a damn about hurting Phoenix's feelings. But she's Atlas' mother. She will always be his mother. I can't do that to her.

I shake my head and finally pull myself out of his grasp. I'm still trapped in my seat, boxed in beneath his arm.

"Phoenix needs to face reality." He tilts his head as a lock of his hair falls into his eyes. I want to reach up and swipe it out of his eyes, but I remain motionless.

"What do you mean?"

He huffs. "I asked her for a divorce."

I blink. I must have imagined him. There is no way he wants to divorce Phoenix. She's the mother of his children.

"Don't act like you didn't hear me. I asked Phoenix for a divorce."

"And…" my voice cracks. "What did she say?"

"Phoenix and I are getting a divorce as soon as this is all over."

"Sure, you are. And I'm going to be the next Queen of England."

His eyes roam down my body. "You'd make one hot as fuck queen."

I roll my eyes.

And then his lips graze my cheek.

"What are you doing?"

"Getting you to tell me the truth or fucking you in the back of this jet. The choice is yours."

I swallow, but the lump in my throat barely moves. My

palms sweat, and my body tingles. I'm not going to survive his form of torture.

I should just give in and fuck him. Everyone already thinks I'm a bitch who steals other people's men. Phoenix certainly does. I might as well live up to my reputation.

I have a wicked soul that's been hardened by years of pain. I'll do enough horrible things with what remains of my life. I don't have to hurt Phoenix. Not like this.

"I'm not telling you anything, and you aren't fucking me either."

His tongue flicks over my earlobe, causing my lips to part and moan.

"You can pretend you have control over your body all you want, but it's not the truth. The truth is you and I were made for each other. We've resisted for years because we knew that if we ever gave in, we would never stop. Now that we've had each other, there is no stopping the inevitable. You can't stop us from happening. Phoenix can't. None of our enemies can. We are meant to be together, huntress."

"We hate each other, killer. That will never change. Being together hurts too many people."

He kisses down my neck to my clavicle. "I didn't mention anything about love. All I said was we belong together. We belong hating each other. Fighting together. Fucking together. Our lives became more intertwined than either of us ever expected. The second I tore your father's letter out of your hand all those years ago, you and I became an 'us.'"

My eyes are trained on the ceiling as my mouth parts. I breathe heavily through my mouth as his hand pushes up my shirt, his fingers walking up my stomach.

He's right—love may not be in the cards for us, but everything else is fair game.

I'm a horrible, sinful bitch.

"Talk to me, huntress, and this stops." He kisses the

corner of my mouth as his hand continues to climb higher on my body until he's cupping my breast.

I suck in a breath as his thumb brushes over my nipple. My eyes dart to Phoenix.

Please, god, let her be blasting her music and not look back here.

"I can't."

He grins against my lips. "Can't or don't want to?"

I gasp, and then his mouth is on mine. I try to close my mouth, but I'm not fast enough. His tongue is in my mouth; his lips hungrily eat mine. My mind is mush as he devours me.

Can't.

Don't want.

Definitely want.

My hand grabs his neck as I deepen the kiss. I denied wanting Langston for so long that every time I kiss him, I think it's a dream. It can't be real. None of this is real.

But then his tongue dances across mine, he lets a throaty growl out, his hand pinches my nipple, and I realize just how real it is. As real as all of the horrible things I've ever experienced.

Langston's hands start moving lower off my breast and down my stomach as he continues to attack my mouth, using his tongue as a weapon.

"Talk to me, huntress, or I'm going to fuck you with my fingers until you scream so loud that Phoenix will hate you forever."

"You wouldn't."

He grins. "Let's see how quiet you can be when I give you an orgasm that shatters every nerve ending in your body."

I gulp.

My eyes drift to Phoenix. *Maybe it's for the best that she hates me?* We don't need to get along. We both just have to play our roles in protecting our children.

No!

Get ahold of yourself. You're better than this.

His hands keep traveling south, and I only have moments to decide. I don't have much strength in telling Langston no, but I'll have none left once his hands reach my pants.

He kisses me again, and I moan, quickly losing my ability to control this situation. I'd rather him be holding a gun; I'd have a better shot at defeating him than with his tongue in my mouth.

I don't know which way Langston would rather me choose either—telling him the truth or letting him fuck me until I lose control. Whatever I choose, he wins.

Forgive me, Phoenix.

We were always doomed to become nemeses. My cousin, who gets to love the boy I grew up with freely. She carried his child, got him to put a ring on her finger and vow eternity to her. I know he says that he wants to get divorced, but when it comes down to it, Langston is an honorable man. He won't divorce Phoenix unless she agrees.

With every tantalizing kiss, I'm becoming more and more of the tragic whore I was always destined to become. I'm the thorn in his side. The darkness that overshadows his children and brings the monsters in the night.

I may be the cheater, but I won't be the monster that brings children anymore suffering. It's just one of the many reasons that Langston and I are not meant to be together. He's wrong—we don't belong together in any way. Our lives have become intertwined because of that damn letter that he stole from me and because fate played a sick game on us by having Langston adopt my child.

Knowing that every kiss we exchange is going to break our hearts that much more when this ends doesn't stop the kisses. It doesn't stop our teeth from clashing, our tongues from wrestling, and our moans from escalating.

Each kiss brings me further away from reality. I forget to be quiet to prevent Phoenix from hearing, and I no longer flail my arms in failed attempts to push him away. Instead, my fingers curl around the neck of his shirt, holding him tight against me so I can invade his mouth with my tongue.

His fingers continue to drag down my flat stomach filled with enormous butterflies that build into a swarm of feelings that I'm never going to be able to decipher.

"I want this," I say as his hands lower.

We both lock eyes. I expect a cocky grin; instead, he gives me a seductive gaze that has my insides melting. His hand finds the top of my jeans and begins to unbutton them. We've stopped kissing, both intensely focused on what his hand is doing.

This is wrong.

So wrong.

But my whole life has been wrong. After this is over, I may regret the pain I've caused, but right now, I just want this man—the only man left in the world that I trust to make me feel good.

"Can you be quiet, huntress?"

I nod as his hand pushes beneath the fabric of my jeans and cups my sex. I moan loudly, before realizing my mistake and biting down on his shoulder to keep from making another sound.

He chuckles. "I'm not going to let you be quiet. I'm going to make you scream until the pilot comes back here thinking he needs to make an emergency landing."

"Your fingers aren't that good."

His scruff rubs against my cheek as his tongue tickles the rim of my ear. "Liar. Everything about me is that good—

fingers, tongue, cock. I'm going to make you scream my name with each one."

All of my brain cells burst with his deeply arrogant words. I slant my head as I resume kissing him. I no longer remember why I don't want to make a sound, just that I don't. Kissing him muffles any sounds that escape. He's right; I will moan, groan, and scream every time he touches my clit or pushes himself inside me.

His fingers push aside my panties and spread my lips before dipping inside.

I moan around his bottom lip that I've pulled into my mouth and sucking ferociously, trying to control myself.

"So wet for me already."

His fingers push further inside me, spreading me and making me feel whole. His thumb brushes over my clit.

I bite down with everything I can—using his lip like someone might bite down on a belt in olden days when they are about to lose a limb. Langston is doing the same to me—except instead of losing a limb, I'm losing my soul.

His thumb is merciless as he rubs faster and faster on my clit until water stings my eyes from trying to keep my screams inside. I taste his blood in my mouth, but he doesn't surrender. It seems he's happy to pay the price in blood to make me pay in sin.

I crumple as his fingers thrust in and out, crushing all my walls I've built to keep him out.

His hand slides down my back before he dips me sideways in our row of seats until I'm lying on my back. He settles between my spread legs, his hand still inside me, but our mouths separated. I no longer have his lip to bite down on, nothing to muffle my cries.

He smirks down at me, knowing once again that he's won.

Why did I need to keep quiet again?

With one hand still inside me, his other hand moves to my stomach, pushing my shirt up before running down my center. Then his fingers dip lower, tracing over my C-section scar.

A scar he has avoided touching or commenting on until now.

My scar.

Atlas.

I prop myself up on my elbows abruptly, pushing through the fog that has surrounded my head since he started touching me.

"Stop."

He does, but he doesn't remove his fingers from my slit.

"We can't." I shake my head. "I'm already a cheater, a whore, a bitch. And as bad as my body wants me to become a cheater again, we can't. I won't hurt Phoenix. I won't hurt the mother of my child. Before, I thought we were going to die. Now, we have a choice. I won't make the same mistake again."

My breathing is erratic, and my hands shake. My entire body is calling me a fool for telling Langston to stop.

"Tell me what you're hiding, or I keep going," Langston says with a devilish smirk.

"You wouldn't."

"Try me."

My breath hitches, and my heart rate skyrockets. *How do I get out of this with my body and sanity intact?*

Tell him the truth—at least what you can of it. Tell him the why.

"You tell me I should trust you. That we are on the same side—both looking for the treasure and a way to protect our kids."

He nods.

"I trust you," I say.

His eyes widen at my admission.

"And now I'm asking you to trust me. I can't tell you any more than I already have. At least not yet. It's not safe."

"Not safe for who?"

"For you! Our kids need a father alive."

He pauses, and I'm not sure what he's going to do—keep torturing me to tell him the truth or let this go.

Slowly, he slides his fingers out of me. He pushes my panties back in place and even zips up my jeans and fastens the button.

Then he lifts his fingers to his lips and sucks my juices off them. I'm so close to coming that I'm afraid just watching this enchanting man suck his fingers is going to make me come, so I look away.

"They also need their mother to stay alive," he says as he holds out his hand to me.

I take it, and he helps me sit back up.

"They already have a mother," I say, my eyes locking on the back of Phoenix's head. She's still looking straight ahead, and I have no idea if she knows what happened between us.

He stands up and looks at me sadly. "Maybe they need two."

8

LANGSTON

That's what Liesel wants—trust.

I sink back into my chair next to Phoenix. She doesn't even glance up from her phone. She can pretend she doesn't know what I went back to Liesel for all she wants, but pretending we are one big happy family isn't going to make our children's lives any better. We have to face the truth.

Liesel said she trusts me. I assume that must be true since she didn't immediately demand her child be removed from my custody. To some extent, she must also trust Phoenix.

But do I trust her?

I want to. I want to trust her desperately. I want to trust that everything I thought I knew about Liesel isn't true—that she didn't do the horrible thing I discovered. I want to believe that the reason she's hiding things from me is truly to protect our kids. I want to trust her.

But I don't.

She's broken my trust so many times, as have I.

I don't know why she's changed her mind and now trusts me. Or maybe that's a lie, like everything else she speaks.

63

I do know that we have to figure out a way to trust each other if we are going to survive this; I just don't know how.

Phoenix finally looks at me and smiles weakly as she puts the hood of her hoodie up over her head and then leans on my shoulder, her hand resting against my inner thigh. It doesn't bother me how blasé she is with touching me. Phoenix has earned the right to touch me however she wants.

The problem is I don't crave her touch. I crave the spicy blonde in the back who wants to castrate me as much as she wants to fuck me. The woman hates as much as she loves me. The woman who is mine and yet will never actually be mine.

When Liesel told me to stop, I thought I was imagining it. There was no way I could be feeling like I felt touching her, and her have the capacity to tell me to stop. The burning desire bolting through me was buzzing through her body too. I saw it in her hooded eyes, her parted lips, and the way she bit down on my lip.

I tortured her with my body not because I actually thought it would lead her to tell me the truth, but because I needed something to ground myself in her again. I thought she needed the same—an escape from reality together.

But then she asked me to stop.

Does she have more control over her urges than I do? Or is her lust just not as strong as mine is?

I move my head, and a drop of blood splotches Phoenix's cheek. Her thumb swipes across her pale cheek, and then she looks at the red-colored liquid on the tip of her thumb.

I don't know how she's going to react to seeing evidence of my interactions with Liesel. I watch curiously as she waits a beat before placing her thumb into her mouth, sucking the blood off.

Nothing.

A sight like that in the past might get me hard and horny as hell. I'd be pulling her into the nearest bathroom to fuck her senseless. That was who I used to be—a horny bastard content on fucking everyone.

My eyes sear back to where I left my heart—sitting next to Liesel, my huntress.

Phoenix sits up and examines me closer until she finds the source of the blood—my bottom lip. A lip that Liesel bit down on to keep from screaming my name as I fucked her with my fingers—fingers that still smell like her.

Phoenix's eyes glaze over into a frosty shade. I can see the damn icicles hanging from her eyelashes.

I prepare myself for her slap, bite, hit, rage. I deserve it. Even though we have an open marriage, I know that I hurt her. I hate hurting her. She's one of my closest friends, and I'll always owe the world to her. I married her never thinking I'd want another woman as a constant in my life. I was wrong, but so was Phoenix for thinking that she could make me fall in love with her.

The slap never comes. Instead, she leans close to my lips, uncomfortably close, until we are sharing oxygen.

"Dunn," I warn.

"You vowed your body to me forever. I let you fuck other whores, but you will always be mine. We aren't getting a divorce. You don't want that. You're just confused by old feelings. You want me."

I shake my head, careful not to let our lips brush against each other.

"She hurts you." Her thumb brushes over my swollen, bleeding lip. "I heal you."

And then she presses her lips against mine. She might call it a kiss, but for it to be a kiss, I'd have to kiss her back. That doesn't stop her. She licks her tongue over my wound, trying to heal me with her saliva.

I give her one more second to get whatever jealousy she's feeling toward Liesel out of her system. Then, I grab her shoulders and hold her back.

She tilts her head, her brows pulling together.

"Stop," I say, repeating the word that Liesel said to me.

"You're my husband. You don't get to tell me to stop. You're mine."

I shake my head. "I was never yours. We have an agreement on paper to protect the kids; that's all. I care about you deeply, Dunn. And that's why I'm going to spend the rest of the flight in the cockpit."

I stand up before I release her.

"Baby, please," she begs.

"I care about you. I'm sorry for hurting you, but I can't, Dunn—not anymore. I'm sorry."

And then I walk to the cockpit. I don't allow myself to glance back at either of the women. I don't want to see the pain I'm causing both of them.

All I know is I'm a stupid man who thought I'd never care about a woman more than I do Phoenix. I wasn't sure I had a heart. Even Siren thought I'd never fall in love and agreed that marrying Phoenix was for the best.

Then Liesel came back into my life and fucked up all my plans.

———

I got the silent treatment from both women during the entirety of our landing and drive to our hotel. The sky is dark, so we won't be searching for any treasure tonight.

I park the rental car in front of the swankiest hotel I could find. I chose the best not because I need us to rest in luxury, but because expensive hotels have the most cameras to hack into ensuring our safety.

Phoenix continues to give me an icy glare from the passenger seat next to me. Liesel stares out the window, completely lost in thought like we aren't even here at all. If Liesel is upset that Phoenix kissed me, she's not showing it.

I get out of the car, scanning every person on the street, my gun at my back, my fingers tingling to grab it. After the explosion at my house, I don't trust that we aren't being followed.

A couple walks by holding hands, and my mind immediately goes to them being dangerous. A woman is carrying a baby in one hand while holding the hand of a crying toddler with the other—an obvious enemy in my paranoid mind.

Liesel steps out of the car, her eyes scanning just like mine, searching for the devil inside every person who walks by.

Another door slams. Phoenix struts by us and walks through the automatic doors of the hotel, her anger overtaking any fear she has.

Liesel and I exchange a glance wordlessly, and then we walk inside.

"Do you still have a gun?" I ask.

She nods.

"Good girl."

She rolls her eyes. "That's not going to work. You can't seduce me by saying things like 'good girl.'"

"I'd bet everything I own that your panties are wet right now." I wink at her.

Her ears pink, and I know I'm right.

We hit the lobby floor, and our flirting stops. People are milling about everywhere—the reception desk, the lounge, the bar. People walk briskly past us and danger could be anywhere.

"Stay close," I order.

She nods, walking next to me. Phoenix emerges from the

bar with a dry martini in her hand as she settles into a walk on my left.

"Don't leave my side again, Dunn."

Both women look at me. I should really stop calling Phoenix, 'Dunn.'

"Why? Miss me already?" Phoenix bats her eyelashes at me as she grips my arm.

"Just do what I say so you don't end up dead."

Phoenix gasps and then grips my arm tighter as I walk up to the reception desk.

"How can I help you, sir?" the man behind the desk asks.

"Can I get a suite with two adjoining rooms?"

I don't have to turn my head to feel the two sets of eyes from each woman burning into my side.

"I want my own room," Liesel says.

"Me too," Phoenix huffs.

"Two adjoining rooms or a suite with two bedrooms and a couch," I say to the gentleman.

"We have a suite with two queen bedrooms and a spacious living room pull out couch."

"Perfect."

I pull out cash to pay. I don't want anything tied to our names revealing our location. The man slides me three room keys.

"Can we talk? I don't think it's a good idea for the three of us to share a suite," Phoenix says, tugging on my arm.

"If we want to all stay alive, it is."

I look over to Liesel, expecting more of a fight from her as well, but her eyes are scanning the crowd.

My eyes follow her gaze. *Does she sense some danger that I'm not seeing?*

Carefully, I position Phoenix behind me as I put my hand on my gun.

"What is it?" I ask Liesel.

She smiles.

I frown.

She starts running excitedly in the direction of the bar.

"Looks like I don't have anything to worry about after all," Phoenix says, stepping next to me again as she sips her martini.

Liesel jumps into the arms of a man in a suit and jealousy rears its head inside me. So much so, that it takes me a second to recognize the man whose arms she flung herself into.

Maxwell.

I thought we had agreed that he was too shifty to be trusted, but she's acting like she just met up with a long lost friend.

I hand Phoenix a room key. "Go to the room and don't leave."

"Why? I want to watch the show."

"Dunn," my voice is serious and commanding, so Phoenix will do as I say. That's one of the traits I can always count on with her. When our lives hang in the balance, all I have to do is give her an order, and she'll follow it. Phoenix rolls her eyes and saunters toward the elevators.

I walk over to Maxwell and Liesel, my hands itching to grab the gun, but I don't since we're in a crowded lobby. That won't stop me from killing this bastard, though.

"Get your hands off her," I growl at Maxwell.

He doesn't budge an inch. His hand remains on the small of her back. His rigid, clean-cut appearance does nothing to make me trust him. That's why he appears the way he does in a suit and tie; he looks like a trusted businessman instead of the scum I know he is.

"Langston, it's so nice to see you again."

"Let her go," I roar through gritted teeth.

He chuckles. "Liesel is the one who called me. I'm not

holding her hostage." He waves his hand, showing he has no weapon pressed against her back. "I'm here to help her."

"It's the truth. I called him," Liesel says.

"And why the hell would you do that?" I spit in her face. *How dare she pull a move like this without talking to me first!*

Her eyes implore me to trust her, but we've already established that I don't.

"Waylon wasn't the one in charge at his organization. He was second in line. The man in charge is still after me. He still demands that I give him what he wants. Now that Waylon's dead, he's impatient. He wants this over. Maxwell has met him before. I told him to meet us here so we could talk to him about what he knows," Liesel says, giving me more information that was in that damn letter.

She's lying. Or at least, she's hiding something—*from me or from Maxwell?* That's the question.

"What is this man's name?" I ask Maxwell.

"Corbin."

I square myself, looking at Maxwell. He has a couple of inches on me. At first glance, it would seem he has bigger muscles than me. But he doesn't know I grew up fighting Zeke, the biggest, physically strongest man I know. I know how to fight hulks, and I know how to win.

I want to order Liesel to go to the suite, so I can beat Maxwell's ass into telling me everything he knows before I kill him. But I know that she will never allow that.

Instead, I flag down a waitress.

"Table for three, please."

She smiles at the three of us. "Right this way, please."

We sit at a table near the bar, surrounded by people. The only good thing about sitting at a restaurant this crowded is that Maxwell is less likely to make a move.

We each order a drink, and then I say, "Start talking."

9

LIESEL

THE VEIN on Langston's forehead is bulging as he glares at Maxwell. I'm surprised Langston hasn't already climbed across the table and strangled him. Right now, all of his anger is focused on Maxwell, but soon his intimidating glare will turn toward me. But he won't do it, not as long as Maxwell, the bigger threat, is sitting at the table.

Langston doesn't know why Maxwell is really here. I'm not even sure why he's here. Call it a hunch. After I got the threatening note, I knew that Waylon was behind it.

I just didn't know if somehow Waylon was alive or if it was someone working for Waylon or this Corbin guy who sent the threat. It was a risk bringing Maxwell here—a huge risk—but my gut says Maxwell might be the only way to get the truth.

I understand why Langston is practically growling and shooting daggers at Maxwell. Langston has no idea if Maxwell is on Waylon's side or ours, and when our kid's lives are at stake, you don't let anyone into our lives that could threaten theirs.

What annoys me is that Langston has yet to show that he trusts me.

After everything we've been through together. After fucking each other. After learning he's raising my son. After all of it, he still doesn't trust that I would never do anything I think could hurt us, any of us—Langston, Phoenix, or our kids.

Maxwell's gaze turns to me, waiting for me to tell him where to start. He's here for me, not Langston.

I open my mouth just as the waitress brings over our drinks on a tray. Our silence stretches as the woman places three scotches in front of us. I give her a tight smile but don't offer a thank you. The air is too intense for any of us to mumble a word that could be seen as a weakness to the others at the table. The waitress senses something is off about the three of us and scurries off as fast as she can.

We return to our staring contest. Langston glares at Maxwell, while Maxwell stares at me. And I am torn between the two men.

"Waylon is dead, correct?" I ask, deciding to start with what I think will be an easy question for Maxwell to answer. In our world, people die and then come back to life. I basically faked Siren's death. It wouldn't be impossible that Waylon did the same.

Except, Langston was the one who killed Waylon, and there would be no reason for him to fake that. Plus, I was the one who discovered Waylon. He was covered in blood and had no pulse. Unless he has an identical twin or he has literal powers to return from the dead, he's dead.

"Waylon is dead," Maxwell says.

Both Langston and I study him closely, looking for any tell that he's lying. When you've been lied to by people as often as Langston and I have, you learn to read people better than most.

"So if Waylon didn't send me that threatening note, who did?" I ask.

Maxwell drinks down his entire glass, like he needs courage for the next part.

"Corbin, his brother."

I narrow my eyes. "Waylon doesn't have a brother. He's an only child."

"He has a brother."

"And how do you know that?" Langston asks, gripping his glass hard so he doesn't punch Maxwell in the face.

"He's the one who hired me," Maxwell answers.

My breathing stops, and for a second, I think I made a mistake bringing Maxwell here. I let him get close to the next clue that could lead us to the treasure.

Langston's leg bounces under the table, and I grab it, trying to get him to calm the fuck down.

He doesn't so much as glance my way. He just shakes my hand off his thigh and keeps bouncing like I'm nothing more than an annoying fly that just landed on his leg.

"Tell me why I shouldn't kill you right now," Langston says in a low, deep voice.

"Without me, you won't be able to find him."

Langston laughs. "I'm sure I can figure it out."

It's then that I realize Langston has his gun trained on Maxwell underneath the table.

Maxwell senses it too, but he doesn't seem concerned. He makes no move to get up, to defend himself. Instead, he looks at me with warm eyes.

"Waylon's brother hired me to keep you safe, Liesel. My job is still to protect you. Whether my loyalty lies with him or you, it doesn't matter. I'm your only shot at staying safe."

"Like hell you are! I'm her only shot at staying safe," Langston says.

Maxwell ignores Langston and keeps looking at me.

"I was sent to blow up the house, killing everyone but Liesel to send a message that he can get to you any place at any time if you don't cooperate. I chose to wait until you were all out."

He shouldn't have said that. Now he's a dead man, and there is nothing I can do to protect him.

I can feel Langston boiling next to me, itching to drag this man into an alley and kill him.

"He has your son, Liesel. He knows where he is. Waylon wasn't lying about that."

I don't react. I don't want Maxwell to be able to read me at all. I don't want him to know that I don't believe him because Langston is the one who has my son. And he's currently safe in hiding with Beckett.

Maxwell smirks, though, thinking he has the key to getting us to do whatever he wants.

"That's not a reason for me to keep you alive. That's a reason for me to kill you," Langston says.

"I know. I didn't realize that a child was involved. If I did, I would have never agreed to work for him. The money was good, and with my criminal record, I couldn't get a job that paid half as well. After I learned they're holding a child hostage to get you to do what they want, I vowed I would do whatever I could to protect you both. Believe me or not, but I'm here to help you, Liesel."

It doesn't matter if I believe him or not. I won't let another man risk my child's life.

"Prove it. Tell me everything about Corbin. Tell me where my son is," I say. My eyes connect with Maxwell's. I plead with him to stop hiding the truth from me.

"His name is Corbin Brown. He's two years older than Waylon. He inherited his father's drug smuggling organization and doubled it in size. While Waylon, being the much more charming and less evil of the two, decided getting law enforcement and government in his pocket was the best way to help the business instead of handling the day to day organization. So he ran for office. They also had a third brother. He was the youngest. He was killed in a shoot-off with a rival organization just before his eighteenth birthday. And a sister, who I don't think involves herself in the illegal stuff."

I bite my lip, and my heart aches for Waylon. He had two brothers. One dead. The other a criminal.

"Both men wanted a way to increase their power and money so they would never have to worry about losing one of their own again. They heard of this legend from your father, Liesel. More money than they earned in the last decade. That kind of money would give them the power to never be threatened again. So they worked together to get you under their control. Waylon courted you, while Corbin took your son. You were the key to getting everything they ever wanted. With Waylon's murder, nothing will stand in the way of Corbin doing whatever it takes in order to get you to give him the treasure. Nothing."

The concern in Maxwell's eyes feels real, too real. He's either a good actor, or he truly is concerned for my son's life. My son, who is perfectly safe. *But if my son is with Beckett, whose child does Corbin mistakenly have?*

"Why are you here telling me all of this? I've been trying to figure out who Waylon works with for months," I say.

"Because I made a mistake working for them, and I want to help fix that."

Langston scoffs, like it's not possible.

"Tell me where Corbin is keeping my son," I say.

Maxwell's eyes water. "I don't know."

"You're a dead man," Langston says.

"No! He's not." I slam my hand down on the table, getting the attention of an older couple nearby who looks at me in disgust for my inappropriate outburst. I don't care, though. My outburst got the attention of the two men.

"I don't trust you, Max, but I haven't sentenced you to death yet either. What did Corbin tell you to do?"

"My assignment is to convince you to trust me, that I'm on your side, and to keep you safe. To help you get the treasure and then convince you to give it to Corbin in exchange for him keeping your child safe." His eyes lighten with the truth.

His words may be true, but are his intentions?

"You're only helpful to me alive if you can help me figure out where my son is. Is that something you can do?"

"Yes, that's all I want. I don't want an innocent child hurt. I would never knowingly work for a man who would do that."

"Killer," I say, rubbing Langston's arm, trying to calm him down. But the second my fingers graze his muscular bicep, I feel the zing of electricity. This time it isn't attraction between us—it's rage flowing freely off his skin.

"We are going to search him, find any bugs, any electronics he could be using to send back to Corbin. Then we are going to tie him up in our suite until we get all the information we can from him. Understood?" I ask Langston.

I'm not sure he heard me, but then Langston nods his head the slightest amount in agreement. I doubt he agrees with my plan. I'm sure he wants to kill Maxwell, but we have to keep him alive. We have no leads on Corbin. And he has a child hostage. I have no doubt that Atlas is my son, but Corbin is holding an innocent child thinking he's mine. We have to do something to save the child and stop him from discovering Atlas. Maxwell is the only lead we have.

Langston digs some cash out of his wallet and throws it on the table.

"After you," he says to Maxwell.

Maxwell and I both stand. Maxwell keeps his eyes on Langston. I turn my head back and forth between the two men, trying to get a read on either of them. They seem to be playing a silent game between themselves I don't understand.

Without a word, we walk out of the bar. Maxwell in front, followed by Langston, and then me trailing them both.

Maxwell walks to the elevator banks and presses the up button, while Langston and I flank his either side. If he plans to run, we'll stop him. I still have the gun I took from Langston's car. I have no problem shooting this man.

The doors open, and we all step into the lift. Langston presses the fifth-floor button, waits for the elevator to rise, then presses the emergency stop button. Langston turns to Maxwell with his arms crossed as he stands in front of the door.

The corner of Maxwell's mouth lifts, and then he starts pulling out his phone, gun, wallet, and watch. He flings each on the floor at Langston's feet.

Maxwell raises his eyebrows. "Satisfied?"

"No, not until you're dead." Langston walks over to Maxwell and starts patting him down, looking for any other electronic device on him. When he's finished, he walks back to his place in front of the doors.

"Does Corbin know where we are?" Langston asks.

Maxwell shakes his head. "I told him I was going to Patagonia and just had a layover for tonight in Peru."

"I don't have anything with me to scan you to see if you have a tracking device in your body, but if you are lying to us and still communicating with Corbin in any way, you'll wish I killed you here on this elevator," Langston growls.

Maxwell nods. "I wouldn't expect anything less."

Suddenly, Maxwell seems smaller. Anyone else might see them as two alphas fighting for power over the situation. In reality, Langston is always the alpha, always in control.

Langston fists his hand and slams it over the emergency stop button. The elevator starts creeping up again until we reach our floor. This time Langston motions for me to step out first, so I do. I walk to our room and insert my key.

As soon as all three of us are in the room, Langston turns on Maxwell and attacks him viciously. A fist flies in Maxwell's face before he can react, followed by a swift kick to his ankles, knocking him on the mahogany-colored carpet.

Langston is on top of him a second later, pulling Maxwell's arms behind his back roughly.

"Get me something to tie him up with," Langston says to me.

Just then, Phoenix exits one of the bedrooms in a robe while carrying a martini glass. Her eyes pop. "I thought I had to come up here because it wasn't safe for me down there. But you all just brought the danger up anyway."

I ignore Phoenix. I need to find something to tie up Maxwell with.

I start opening cabinets, digging through drawers trying to find something to use. I walk over to an end table, yank a phone cord out of the wall, and toss it to Langston.

Langston snatches the cord mid-air and then ties Maxwell's wrist together so tightly I'm afraid that he's going to amputate his wrists. He grabs Maxwell by the collar and forces him to his feet.

I feel concern for Maxwell. He's protected me before, looked out for me, and if he's telling the truth, he doesn't deserve to be treated this way. I called him here for a reason. I just can't figure out what that reason is yet, what my instincts were screaming at me to get Maxwell here for. Then Maxwell winks at me, and my concern vanishes.

Langston marches him through the suite to one of the bedrooms. He slams the door shut until it's just me and Phoenix both standing awkwardly in the living room, staring at each other.

"So I take it he's not on our side?" Phoenix asks.

I shrug. "We don't know."

Phoenix shakes her head. "I don't know what it is about you that makes Langston fall over his feet to do whatever you say."

"He doesn't do that."

She scoffs. "He does. Because if what you are saying is true and that man isn't on our side, then Langston would shoot him dead, not tie him up."

The bedroom door opens, and Langston remerges. He stares me down, shooting daggers my way as he motions for me to come with him. He walks into the other bedroom. I follow.

As soon as I'm inside the room, Langston slams the door behind me before slamming me against the door, his hand at my neck as he squeezes.

"Tell me what the hell is going on right now, or I'm going to fuck it out of you."

10

LANGSTON

I'VE NEVER BEEN SO furious with Liesel in my life, and that's really saying something as I'm always angry with her. She brought the enemy with her. We ran, and she left a trail for the enemy to follow. He blew up my house, threatened my children, and she invited him here for drinks.

My hand grips her neck, while I try to decide between strangling her to death or fucking her. *No, it's not a decision— I want to fuck her to death.*

Liesel's lips part, and her tongue settles between her teeth. Her breath is slow and steady, unlike her raging pulse. She wants me to believe that she's relaxed in my grip, but her heart says otherwise. She's either scared shitless, turned on, or both.

"It was a hunch," she whispers through her parted lips.

"What?"

"A hunch, that's why I told Maxwell where we were. That's why I told him to come here. My gut told me he's the key to bringing Corbin down."

"You're a foolish woman."

She licks her lips. "And you're a wicked man."

81

I move in close to her until my mouth is hovering over hers, but I'll deny us both kisses. This isn't about pleasure. This is about getting answers for my brain and wetness for my cock.

I grab her bottom lip, sucking it into my mouth and biting down hard.

She doesn't wince. Her eyes bore into mine, enjoying the pain.

"Tell me why you made the horrible, fucking wrong decision to bring Maxwell here without talking to me first. Or I'm going to fuck you so hard my wife and the entire hotel will know you're mine."

"I don't belong to anyone. I'm a loner. You can't have a wife and have me."

I grin. "Good, because soon I won't have a wife. I'll only have you."

I tug on her bottom lip again until it's swollen and red. "What was on that note?"

"Nothing."

I grab her by the waist, spin her, and slam her back hard against the dresser. My hands snake down the sides of her body, and I watch delicious goosebumps pop up on her smooth skin.

"Why. Is. He. Here?"

"I told you—a hunch. Waylon's brother sent the note, and I've always suspected Maxwell was pretending to be a little incompetent as a bodyguard. I sensed something deeper in Maxwell, something I don't understand. So I lured him here, away from the kids. Now, we can get the information we need from him and then kill him."

"Or we could just kill him."

She shoves me hard in the chest, pushing me off her body.

I think she's going to run away, but she surprises me. She

sprints at me until I'm falling back on the bed. Her legs land on either side of my waist as she reaches for her gun and aims it at my heart.

"No, we can't kill him—not yet. Not until he's told us everything."

She grinds her hips over mine, and my cock springs up against the zipper of my jeans, trying to get to her.

She wants to play—dirty and rough. She won't back down and let me control her. She won't let me use sex as a weapon. She's willing to throw it right back at me.

"I won't let you make me feel bad for wanting to fuck you. I'm not a nice woman, never have been. I'm thankful to Phoenix for raising my child. But if I fuck you, I won't be the one cheating—you will be. If that's how you want to repay the woman you owe everything to, then so be it. But I'm not going to let your threats get to me."

My jaw ticks looking at the sexiest woman in the world straddling me with a gun in her hand like she's completely in control. It's adorable that she thinks that. My heart beats faster, though, because maybe she's right. She's more in control of this situation than I am.

"You don't know what you're talking about. Phoenix fucks who she wants, same as me. An open relationship is not cheating."

"Oh, Phoenix is okay with you fucking me?"

"Yes."

She shakes her head with a smug expression. "Now, who's lying?"

I toss her off and roll onto her as I fling the gun out of her hand. She growls, and I pin her hands over her head, my hard body slamming into every part of her softness.

"Maxwell has to die," I say.

"You don't get to make that decision."

"Just like you don't get to make the decision to bring him here without consulting me first."

I come down hard on her lips—getting a taste of her fiery sweetness before sudden pain overtakes me.

I roll off her after she knees me hard in the balls.

She moves to get off the bed, but I grab her shirt. It starts to tear as she reaches for the gun. I throw her back on the bed, ripping her shirt completely off of her.

She gasps when I stare at her bare stomach and kiss her skin above her belly button.

For a moment, she lets me touch her. She strokes my hair as I kiss her tenderly.

We won't be fucking each other tonight, no matter how much we both need it—not with my wife in the next room. Neither of us is that cruel.

I won't be fucking Liesel again until I convince Phoenix to divorce me. Even then, it's a long shot. The only reason she fucked me before is because we thought we were going to die. Now, that time has passed.

Good thing in our world, the threat of death is just around the corner.

I inch up to kiss her breasts, when she slaps me across the cheek.

She grabs my shirt and rips it the same way I did, right down the fucking middle. Her nails dig into my skin next before her teeth bite and nip over my abs.

My eyes roll back in my head with each touch of her mouth against my skin. I shouldn't moan—Phoenix will make me pay for all the sounds I'm making in here, thinking I'm fucking Liesel when I'm not. But dammit, I can't control myself around Liesel.

"Huntress," I warn when her lips lower to just above my pants.

She grins as she continues to kiss down my happy trail.

I grab her chin, lifting her up.

"Don't fight fire with fire," I say.

"Why not?"

"Because I can handle getting burned, but you can't."

"I've been burned before."

"I know—but I can't handle being the one who burns you."

She gasps.

I make my move.

I flip her onto her back and sink my hand back beneath her panties, finding the sweet spot that controls her whimpers, cries, and moans. I rub my finger slowly over her clit, feeling her panties soaking around my fingers.

She's silent at first, and then the first glorious whimper pushes through her luscious lips.

"Please, stop torturing me," she whispers.

I stop.

Her hips buck, begging me to finish her.

My eyes darken. I need answers. I need her to come.

I lean down and kiss her slowly, torturously. It's a real kiss that floods her body with emotions and drenches my hand with her precum.

"Talk to me, huntress. Tell me everything. Trust me with your soul and body." *Trust me with your heart.*

She shakes her head. "Trust me."

My fingers move again over her clit until she can't talk. Her breath is heavy, more gasping than breathing.

A single tear drips down her cheek as I bring her closer to the edge of an orgasm. So close, in fact, that I feel the first ripple before I once again stop.

"I can't," she whispers.

I grit my teeth to keep from slamming my mouth over hers and fucking her senseless.

"But I do know that we can't kill Maxwell, not yet. The child—"

"Isn't yours. Atlas is your child. If you want a DNA test to be sure, we can do that."

"No, I know Atlas is my son. I saw the similarity of our eyes."

"So, Corbin is obviously lying. He doesn't have your child. I have your child. He's safe with Beckett."

"But he has someone's child."

I still, looking at her closely. There have been moments when I'm not even sure she cares about her own child. For her to care about a stranger's child isn't like her.

"You're confusing as hell, huntress."

My fingers dance over her clit again.

Her eyes close as she feels me. She licks her lips and arches her back in ecstasy. One more touch and she'll be screaming my name.

She grabs my wrist, though, stopping me.

"Go back to your wife, killer. You chose her. I'm just a whore you fucked because there was no one else around in the face of death."

I frown. She couldn't be more wrong, but I understand that I caused this mess. I chose Phoenix, and Liesel thinks I still hate her. She doesn't know I've spent my entire life wanting her, dreaming of fucking her.

And now that I've had her, I can't imagine fucking any other woman but her.

11

LIESEL

SLEEP WAS IMPOSSIBLE.

Even though I had my own bedroom and a large queen-sized bed to myself, sleep never came. And neither did I.

After Langston suddenly left, I touched myself. I rubbed furiously while I tried to finish the job Langston started. No amount could bring me to orgasm, though. It's like my body no longer knows how to work without Langston.

I get out of bed as soon as the sun starts rising. My clothes are ripped from Langston, so I walk to the small closet in the room and put on a hotel robe.

My fingers and body wreak of sex. My hair is a mangled mess, but the only way to get to the bathroom to try and tame my hair is to make my way through the common areas. Hopefully, Phoenix and Langston haven't woken up yet. I don't want Phoenix to think I fucked Langston last night. And I don't want Langston to realize I still haven't come.

I open my door carefully, and my eyes peek around the dark room. I don't see anyone.

I creep out, tiptoeing across the room as to not wake anyone.

I make it halfway across the living room before the other bedroom door opens, and Phoenix and Langston stand in the doorway. Phoenix is wearing a robe just like mine. Her hair is bushy on her head, her cheeks warm and pink. Langston stands in nothing but his boxers behind her.

They look like a happy couple.

Phoenix smirks at me.

I know, you won. He's yours. Take him, I don't want him.

It's all a lie. I've never wanted a man more than Langston. But even if Phoenix wasn't in the picture, I could never really have him. I'm the huntress. I have to continue hunting. I've spent my whole life hunting for something that I'm not even sure can be found. And Langston, despite all his faults, is a good man. He doesn't deserve to be dragged down into my despair.

I cut my eyes away from them and dash into the bathroom. I can breathe again as soon as I shut the door. But I know the feeling is only temporary. I relieve myself and am trying to comb through my hair when there's a knock at the door.

"Stop hogging the bathroom. Some of us need to pee, you know," Phoenix says.

Stop being such a pussy, I tell myself before I slap a smile on my face and walk out of the bathroom, past a waiting Phoenix.

"It's all yours," I say.

She steps inside, leaving Langston and me alone.

"Huntress, it's not—"

"You were with your wife last night. I understand. I'm going to make some coffee."

He frowns but doesn't try to explain himself. It's obvious he slept in her room last night instead of the untouched couch. I don't need to know any more details than that.

I refuse to feel jealous as I make the coffee in the small kitchenette area. But the banging I'm making betrays me.

Finally, I finish pouring four cups of coffee.

"Four? Really?" Langston asks.

"Yes, Maxwell gets a cup too."

Langston rolls his eyes.

"Go get him, now."

His lips thin into a single line. For a moment, I think he's going to argue with me, but then he turns and disappears into the bedroom.

He reappears with Maxwell still tied up. He sits him down in one of the living room chairs and then grabs a knife from the kitchen to release his bindings before handing him a cup of coffee.

Maxwell smiles at me as he takes the cup of coffee, knowing this was my doing.

Langston pulls a gun out from the waistband of his boxers.

"If you move, I'll shoot you dead with pleasure," Langston says, casually lifting his cup of coffee to his lips.

"Noted," Maxwell says, drinking his own coffee.

We all sit in the living room in an awkward silence as we drink our coffees. Maxwell in a single chair. Langston and Phoenix are sharing the small loveseat. And me sitting in the other single chair.

"What did I miss?" Maxwell asks, looking between the three of us.

"Nothing. What's the plan?" I look to Langston.

"Oh, now you're going to discuss plans with me? I thought you just made plans on your own," he shoots back.

I sigh. "I have no problem deciding, if you'd rather."

"Will you two stop? The sooner we figure out how to work together, the sooner we can never see each other again," Phoenix says.

"We all go to the sacred ruins, then we get the next clue," I say.

"I already called to have new clothes brought up for us, and a car should arrive in the next twenty minutes," Langston stares back at me.

He didn't argue with me about us all going.

I don't know what to do with that. All I know is that I need to get out of this hotel room before I suffocate in the thoughts of him fucking Phoenix after touching me.

———

Langston rented a six-passenger van and driver to take us to the ruins. The drive is long, winding, and silent.

None of us speak about what we are going to do when we get there. Langston and I don't share any of the information we know about what we might face. We don't discuss what we are going to do with Maxwell or what Phoenix knows.

Eventually, the driver stops and points down a dirt road. Apparently, this is as far as he goes.

Each of us climb out. I feel for my gun, but don't remove it. Just knowing it's there brings some comfort. I'm nowhere near as skilled with a gun as Langston is, but at least I have a weapon to defend myself.

Maxwell asked for a gun, but we refused him. And Phoenix just scoffed when Langston tried to get her to carry a gun.

We all march down the abandoned dirt road, walking as much apart as we are together. If anyone were to notice us, I'm not sure they would be able to deduce if we are a group or four separate strangers. Fog hangs in the air, masking much of the greenery of the surrounding mountains as we continue through the chilly air.

"How much further do we have to hike?" Phoenix pants as the road climbs up the side of the hill.

Langston points to the top.

She sighs.

"I can give you a piggyback ride if you want?" Maxwell asks her.

We all freeze, not sure what Phoenix or Langston is going to do.

Phoenix grins. "Hell yea."

"Dunn, is that a good idea?" Langston asks.

"I'm exhausted. I wasn't made for climbing. So unless you are offering a ride, I'm taking Max here up on his offer."

Langston rolls his eyes and continues climbing. Phoenix climbs on Maxwell's back. I take up the rear.

"You smell good," I hear Phoenix whisper to Maxwell, who chuckles gruffly.

Langston keeps walking like he didn't hear her.

After an hour or more of hiking, we finally reach the sacred ruins.

"Now what?" Phoenix asks, still clinging to Maxwell's back.

Langston stares back at me, like he thinks I have the next clue.

He's right—I do.

My eyes scan the sight. It's beautiful, eery with haze and clouds hanging low in contrast to the bright green grass and broken remains of stone buildings. There are a few tourists and locals milling about, but nothing compared to the hoards of the more famous ruins like Machu Pichu.

"This way," I say, finding a trail to the right of the ruins and following it. I feel Langston fast at my heels as I head down the trail. I expect him to ask me questions about what comes next, but he doesn't. He just follows closely with Maxwell and Phoenix struggling to catch up.

I stop abruptly when I spot the small cottage nestled in the rolling hills.

I look to Langston. I don't know what to do next. He has the next clue.

He walks forward, taking the lead.

I hear Maxwell's feet stopping behind us, and Phoenix climbs off his back.

Langston motions with his head for me to follow him to the side of the house. I do. Maxwell and Phoenix don't follow us.

Langston approaches the small wooden door on the side of the house. He knocks four times and then waits.

My heart is pumping wildly, waiting for what's going to happen next. A minute goes by and nothing happens.

My heart sinks.

This was all a wild goose chase, wasn't it, father? You sent me here to ruin my life.

The door opens.

My eyes widen, and then an older bald man with a white beard steps to the door. He doesn't speak, just stares at Langston.

"A Dunn is here to collect what's hers," Langston says.

The man's eyes go from Langston to me. His eyes look like he's seen a ghost. His ears perk like he can't believe what he just heard.

"You married?" he looks between the two of us, looking for a ring.

My thumb traces my bare ring finger—a finger that will never have a ring.

I look to Langston. He's not wearing a ring either. Weird —I guess I never noticed or thought about it before.

"No," I say.

"I am," Langston says.

The man pokes his head out of the door as if to ask where his wife is then.

"Dunn," Langston calls.

Phoenix steps forward. Her head is proud and boisterous as she saddles up next to Langston, gripping his bicep like she owns him.

She does.

"Come in," he says, opening the door wider for Langston and Phoenix.

They step inside without glancing back at me.

I move to follow, but the old man steps in front of the door, blocking my way.

"Are you married?" he asks.

I shake my head.

"I'm sorry," he says, closing the door.

I step back, staring at the small house as my hand traces down the door. I need to be inside. I need to know what is going on. I need to help keep Atlas safe.

But I'm not married. And for some stupid reason, my father made that a term in finding the treasure.

I walk back to the front of the house, where Maxwell is still standing. I still don't understand his motivations or why I decided to tell him where we are. I'm also surprised he hasn't tried to pull some crap yet.

I hug myself as I stare at the house, trying to decide my next move.

"We could break in. I'm pretty sure we could take that old man," Maxwell says.

I shake my head. I'm sure we could, but it's not getting in that would be the problem. It's getting him to tell us the next clue.

The only way to get inside is if you're married.

I bite my lip, trying to come up with a different way. My eyes cut to Maxwell, hating my plan.

"Fuck this, let's go," I say.

"Where are we going? I thought—"

"We are going to fix our situation so we can get into the house."

12

LANGSTON

WE STEP into the small one-room house. There isn't much to see, but a small bed in the corner with some books strewn over it and a rocking chair in the other corner. This man either lives a simple life or doesn't live here full time.

The door whooshes closed behind us, sinking the room into darkness.

Phoenix jumps, leaning further against me as the room turns pitch-black.

I hear the light of a match striking, and then we can see again as the man walks toward us.

"What's your name?" I ask.

He shakes his head.

I frown. If he isn't even going to tell me his name, I have little faith I'm going to learn much about how to find the treasure.

"I need proof that you two are married." He turns to Phoenix. "And I need your blood."

She shrivels back, using my shoulder to shield herself from him—not that I think she should be worried about such a small, frail man.

I pull out my phone, where I have a saved image of our marriage license, and hand it to him.

He nods, taking the phone from me and sliding it into his pocket. Then he produces a knife and stares at Phoenix, waiting.

She looks up at me. "No."

"Phoenix, he's just going to draw a couple of drops of blood. He's not going to cut off your hand."

She huffs but relents, placing her hand out in front of him. He pricks her finger with the tip of the blade.

He nods his thanks and then disappears out the back door.

"What was that about?" Phoenix asks.

"My guess is he's verifying our marriage license and that you are a Dunn."

She frowns and grips my arm tighter.

I want to tell her to relax. She could be outside with Liesel and Maxwell right now, wondering what the hell is happening and being forced to trust me that I'll tell them what I find out.

I'll tell Liesel everything she needs to know, but I know she's not going to trust a word I say.

The man returns less than a minute after he disappeared.

"I'm sorry, but your marriage isn't valid," he says, handing me back my phone.

"What do you mean it isn't valid?"

I take my phone and stare down at the document that I know is legal.

"It isn't valid."

"How? I mean, what part isn't valid? Do we need to legally marry in this country? Is there some type of ceremony we need to do?"

He shakes his head. "I can't tell you any more other than

you need to leave until you fix the problem. Return once you are truly married."

He walks to the door and opens it.

"But…" Phoenix stutters, just as confused as I am.

I take Phoenix's hand and drag her out the door. I look back one more time at the man who has an intense glint in his eyes. I don't know what just happened, but I'm going to figure it out.

"Liesel, we have a problem…" I stop talking and let go of Phoenix's hand when I round the house and don't find Liesel or Maxwell.

"Liesel?" I shout louder, hoping they just found a more comfortable place to sit and wait for us, but that's not Liesel's style. She would be pacing impatiently just outside the door or looking for a way to break in.

"Where is she?"

A chill creeps down my spine as a thought crosses my mind—a clue to where she might have gone.

Phoenix steps up to my side and rubs my arms in a comforting manner.

"Do you think Maxwell took her?" she asks.

I examine the scene, looking for any sign of a struggle, any sign that Maxwell could have hurt her, but I know better.

"No."

Phoenix narrows her eyes and pulls her brows together as she stares up at me.

"She went to get married so she can enter," I say.

13

LIESEL

I FOUND a small white church in the center of the small town. I've talked with the priest, and he's agreed to marry us. Now, I just have to wait for Maxwell to get back with the paperwork.

I sit in the very last pew, staring up at the stained glass window at the end of the small chapel. The light twinkles as it hits the glass and then flickers into my eyes, making me squint. This doesn't seem real—it feels like a dream, or in reality, a nightmare.

I never wanted to get married. Definitely not to a man who might be more devil than angel. A man I can't imagine kissing, let alone fucking.

We just need to get the paperwork done. That's all this is. A contract that we can eventually annul.

But it won't change the fact that for a short time, I'll be married to Maxwell. I'll promise my life and love to him.

I hear the door open behind me. My eyes water, but I quickly blink them away.

I never imagined myself married. Never thought of myself as a wife or mother. Never wanted the big white dress and lasting love. So marrying a man I don't love just so I can find a treasure shouldn't feel like I'm giving anything up.

But why is my throat tightening, my neck sweating, and my hands clamming up? Why does it feel like I'm losing something I never knew I wanted?

"Ready?" Maxwell asks as he towers over me.

I nod.

He holds out his hand to me.

I try to wipe the sweat off on my pants before I put my hand in his and he helps me stand.

He smiles at me, gently.

"Don't worry, you're still the boss. And I already know there won't be any fucking." He winks at me.

"That's not what I'm worried about. I still don't know if I can trust you."

"You can. I didn't realize who I'm working for. You have my complete loyalty."

I shake my head. "It doesn't matter. You're just a pawn I'm using to get inside that house. You're still our prisoner. I will have no problem killing you when I no longer have a need for you."

He grins. "I have no doubt that you will."

We start walking down the aisle as a woman sits behind a piano and starts playing. The sudden music makes me falter in my step, but Maxwell keeps walking me forward until we are at the altar.

The music stops, and then our priest begins speaking.

I know he's speaking, but I can't hear his words over the beating of my own heart. I can't believe I'm this nervous. All we are doing is speaking meaningless words before we sign a piece of paper.

I close my eyes and steel my heart, forcing it to close tighter than a bank vault. When I open my eyes, I feel strong and ready to do this. Ready to marry this man so I can do what I came here for—to get the damn treasure and protect Atlas in the process.

"Do you take Liesel Dunn—"

"Wait!"

I turn my head and see Langston jogging down the center aisle with Phoenix right behind him.

I blink rapidly.

Langston stops right in front of me, huffing profusely like he ran the whole way here. He doesn't glance at Maxwell; he just grabs my hand and jerks me to the side.

"We'll be right back," Langston mutters as he pushes me out of the side door of the church.

We stumble outside—him out of breath, me not able to breathe. Finally, we come to a stop in a small alleyway between the church and the coffee shop next door.

"What happened?" I ask when I'm finally able to breathe and remove my hand from Langston's grasp.

He growls as I pull away, but he doesn't make a move to take my hand back.

"Don't marry him," Langston says.

I fold my arms across my chest and take a step back. "If you came here to tell me what to do with my life, you can forget it. I don't want to be left out in the dark the next time. I'll marry him, and then we'll kill him. What's the big deal?"

He runs his hand through his hair, and he huffs out a long breath trying to figure out his next words. His eyes are zipping around, crazy with anger.

I don't understand why he's acting this way. It's not like—

"Phoenix and I aren't legally married."

"What?" I gasp.

"We aren't legally married."

"But I saw your marriage license. How could that be?"

He paces a foot. "Some sort of mixup at the registry. He

knew almost immediately that our marriage wasn't valid. I called while we were running over here to verify. It's true—I'm not married to Phoenix."

I nod, slowly, unsure of reality.

"So you didn't get the next clue?"

He shakes his head, slowly mimicking my movements. "No, he kicked us out before he told us anything."

"Stupid father, thinking I need to be married before I get any real money. Like being married will mean I'm somehow protected."

"I don't know why your father thought any of this was a good idea either, but what are we going to do now?"

"I'm going to walk back into the church and get married to Maxwell. You can marry Phoenix for real or not. But at least one of us needs to be married in order to get the next clue."

I take a step toward the church.

He puts his hand on my waist, stopping me from moving. His breath is hot, fire against my lips. I think he's going to say something that will change both of our lives. Something that speaks a lot more of love than of hate.

Instead, he says nothing.

With a twitch of his hand, he pushes our bodies together. Our hips bump, and our mouths land. My eyes close a second later as I taste a man I want but can never have.

This isn't a proposal. He didn't bring me out here to tell me not to marry Maxwell. He knows I have to. He brought me out here for one last goodbye kiss.

Maxwell's and my marriage might be fake, but once we are married, I'm pretty sure the kissing and torturing Langston will have to stop. At least until we get the treasure, since we need the man in charge of hiding the treasure to think I'm married. And after we find the treasure, there is no hope for us.

The sky must agree that this kiss is defiantly wrong in every way as rain starts pouring down on us. It pelts down on us so hard that I can barely breathe. But I'm thankful for the rain because it hides the tears spilling down my cheeks.

Langston notices anyway and rubs my cheeks with his thumbs even though we are both soaked.

I shiver.

"We should go back inside."

He nods.

I start to brush past him, but he doesn't let go of my waist. He doesn't let me move past him.

"Huntress—"

"Don't—you belong with Phoenix."

"But—"

"I was never yours, killer. Let me go."

He does, and I stumble back into the church, sopping wet. Everyone's eyes are on me as I march back to my place in front of Maxwell.

"Where were we?" I ask with a smile.

I RE-ENTER the church through its beaten-down wooden door. I'm soaking wet, and with each step I take inside, I leave a puddle of water behind me. I don't feel the water, though. All I feel is the heat between Liesel and me, even though she's standing far away at the altar with Maxwell.

I walk over to Phoenix in the second pew and sit next to her. Liesel doesn't so much as glance my way. She's staring intently at Maxwell like he's the only man she sees. If a stranger walked into the church right now, they might even deduce from the sight of Maxwell and Liesel together that this is a romantic wedding where the two are so desperate to get married that they can't even wait for her to change clothes.

All I see is the most beautiful woman I've ever met standing in front of the devil about to sign her soul away.

"What's happening?" Phoenix whispers next to me, staring with wide eyes as the priest starts talking again.

"They are getting married." I curse under my breath. "And then we will get married again here."

I don't look at Phoenix to judge her reaction. I'm sure she

has a smug expression on her face, knowing that not only did I marry her once, but I'm going to marry her again. She thinks she's won, that she has a claim over me that Liesel will never have. And yet, I can't stop looking at Liesel.

She will always be mine, even if she's married to another man. She will always be mine.

"I do," Maxwell says.

My heart feels like it's just been hit with a hammer, exploding from two little words. I can't imagine how it's going to feel when she says them.

This is for the best. I can never forgive her—never love her. Getting married is necessary, for both of us.

I try to close my eyes, so I don't have to watch Liesel pledge her life to another man, but I can't seem to force my eyes closed. They are fixated on the tragic nightmare in front of me.

Silence stretches around the room, and I know the priest has just asked Liesel if she takes Maxwell as her husband. All that is left now is for her to answer. For her to reach into my chest cavity and pull out what's left of my disintegrated heart.

"You know they are going to have to fuck, right?" Phoenix says.

I snap my head toward her. "What?"

"That old man will know if their marriage isn't real. They are going to have to consummate the marriage or he'll know. I don't know how, but he seems to know everything. I don't know if this will work if they don't act like a married couple."

"Fuck," I curse. *She's right. I know she is. They are going to have to fuck, to pretend to be in love. And then they'll have to do god knows what in order to get the next clue.*

I glance to Phoenix. I'm going to have to do the same with Phoenix.

This is truly goodbye. I have to let Liesel go. In order to get the treasure, she has to be committed to being married to Maxwell, and I Phoenix. And after all that, she won't want me.

Finally, my eyes are able to close. I slam them shut, sealing myself from the extraordinary pain that only Liesel can cause me. For decades, I've been chasing her—hating her, yet wanting her, knowing how wrong we are for each other, yet assuming we would end up together no matter how wrong it is. In reality, we were destined to get the briefest of moments together and then be lost to another forever.

I keep my eyes closed as a single painful tear escapes. My tear duct takes its time purging the tear, and then the liquid is even slower to descend over my cheek, stopping at each pore to remind me just how painful this moment is.

I hear Liesel breathe, and I open my eyes, knowing this is the moment she says 'I do.' The moment she marries another man.

"Wait!" Phoenix shouts.

I blink, trying to flush the rest of the tears from my eyes so I can figure out if this is a dream or not.

Phoenix pushes me out of the way as she runs up to the altar. She whispers something to Liesel that I can't hear as she takes her hands in hers.

Liesel gasps in shock at whatever she says.

"Are you sure?" Liesel asks.

"More than anything. I was a selfish bitch before."

The two women hug.

I narrow my eyes, trying to understand what the fuck is happening.

Then, Phoenix rushes back to my side. She takes my hand and pulls me out toward the back of the church.

"Wait, I can't leave—"

"Trust me," Phoenix says, yanking me out the doors.

Maybe she's right. Maybe it's for the best I don't want Liesel stomp all over my heart.

We are once again outside in the pouring rain.

"Marry her," Phoenix says.

"What?" I ask.

"Ask Liesel to marry you. You love her or, at the very least, want her. You don't want me. I've done a lot of selfish things in my life. I've stolen you from her and demanded you be mine for years when I have no right. You two belong together. Only the two of you are going to be able to do the tasks required to get the treasure. This is the only way this will work."

I frown. "What about you?"

"I love you. And if I love you, I have to let you go. All I ever wanted to be was a mother, and you gave me that. So I think it's time I return to the thing I love the most—my children."

My heart thumps so loudly in my chest that it blocks out the roar of the thunder.

"You're wrong," I say.

Phoenix looks up at me, even though the rain is pelting down, stinging her cheeks.

"I don't love Liesel. I love you. I'm just not in love with you, Dunn."

"I know." She gives me a weak smile. "But that doesn't change that she's the one you want to marry, not me."

"I'm sorry."

"Don't be. Loving you was one of the best parts of my life."

"I'll love you forever, Dunn."

And then my lips consume hers. It's a kiss that tells her how much I love her. How much I appreciate her. How fucking incredible she is—the most unselfish person I've ever met.

For me, I hope it's a goodbye kiss, but it's also a moment for her to change her mind. If she says she can't give me up yet, that she wants to stay and marry me, then I will. Not because I'm selfless, but because this woman deserves the best man. I'm not the best—but I can give her my best for as long as she wants.

She pushes my chest hard, breaking the kiss.

Her eyes sear into mine—knowing that was a test to see if she can really give me up. The fire in her eyes tells me she can; she already did.

"Go get the girl you love," she whispers.

"I don't love her."

She shakes her head. "Sure, you don't. You can fight it all you want, Langston, but it doesn't make it not true. Stop lying to yourself."

I nod, but I can't, because the only sin I refuse to commit is loving Liesel. Loving her will destroy us both.

15

LIESEL

"WAIT!" Phoenix shouts.

Jesus, if this wedding gets interrupted one more time, I'm not sure I have the guts to go through with it.

Phoenix rushes up and stands between Maxwell and me.

She takes my hands in hers and then whispers, "He's yours. He always has been. I thought I could make him love me, but I was wrong. I won't step in the middle of the two of you again. Being between the two of you doesn't help me; it just means I'll end up getting burned from the inferno you two are bound to create."

"Are you sure?" Liesel asks.

"More than anything. I was a selfish bitch before."

"Thank you," I whisper as she runs back to Langston, dragging him out of the church.

My eyes water once again.

Dammit, I have to stop crying.

"Are we getting married or not?" Maxwell asks me with an annoyance to his voice.

I smile. "No, we aren't."

"Damn, I was sort of looking forward to the honeymoon." He winks at me.

I roll mine.

"Sit your ass down and don't move, or I'll tie you up."

I really should tie him up. Or lock him up. Or kill him. Something. I don't trust Maxwell.

No, you were just going to marry him.

Maxwell sits in the first pew, looking bored.

I wish I knew whose side he was really on and what the hell to do with him. All I know is there is something inside me, a warning bell of sorts that tells me I can't kill him—yet.

I don't know what to do with myself. I want to go outside and talk to Langston, but I should let Phoenix and him have their time.

So I pace.

Back and forth in the front of the altar.

The priest has walked to his back office, realizing this wedding isn't going to happen. It's just me and Maxwell.

"You need to stop doing that," Maxwell says.

"Why?" I keep pacing.

"You have nothing to worry about. That man loves you and will jump at the chance to marry you."

"He can't love me," I whisper more to myself than to Maxwell. I won't let Langston love me.

The door at the back opens, and Langston appears. The sun forms a halo of light around his body as the rain is now nothing more than a pitter-patter behind him.

"Come," he orders.

I hate when he gives me orders. I'm too nervous to protest or ask questions, though, so I walk to him.

"Where is Phoenix?" I ask, looking behind him.

"I got her a car to take her to the jet. She's headed back to watch over the kids."

"I don't think I could have picked a better mother for the

kids than her. She's the most amazing, selfless woman I've ever known. I'll never be able to repay her for everything."

"No, we won't," he agrees.

We stare into each other's eyes as our breathing deepens. I can feel my pulse in my throat—a big, giant heartbeat that wrecks my whole body, taking over every other emotion.

Neither of us speak; we just stare. I'm not sure what to do or what this means.

Are we getting mar—

I can't even finish my own thought in my head, let alone speak it aloud or ask Langston if this means what I think it means.

Langston takes my hand and, without a word, leads me out of the church. Away from the church—that means I was wrong. We aren't getting married.

He moves us quickly, practically running through the streets.

"Where are we going?" I ask.

He doesn't answer. He keeps moving us through town until he stops so suddenly I almost slam into him.

"Wait here," he says, leaving me standing on the side of a road.

He disappears into nearby greenery until I can't see him.

"Langston," I hiss, completely confused by what's happening.

He doesn't answer. He takes his time doing whatever he's doing. Returning a moment later, he wordlessly takes my hand, and then we continue on. The road leads to a hill, but that doesn't stop him. We start climbing up the hillside, both of us still wet from the earlier rain. My feet are going to have blisters from all the walking in wet shoes.

We reach the top of the hill when he stops. I have no idea why, but I turn and look out at the view, and my breath catches. It's stopped raining completely now, a low fog hangs in the air over the town in the Sacred Valley between the mountains, and the sun shines down as if it's shining only on us.

"I hate you," Langston says.

What?

I turn my head toward him, not having a clue what this is all about.

"I hate you, huntress. You've been a thorn in my side since we were kids. You taunted me with your beauty. You tortured me with your smart mouth. You lied to me. Resisted me. Refused to bend to my will. And you hated me in return."

I frown.

He smirks and continues.

"We've both done horrible things—the worst things. Things that can never be forgiven. You're a sadistic princess, and I'm a cruel manwhore. Most of the time I still want to kill you. And yet, we were made for each other."

Only most of the time? I really should ask him why he wants to kill me and why now he only wants to kill me most of the time.

My mouth dries as I gape at him. *What is he doing?*

He bends down on one knee. "I'm not going to say I love you because that would be a lie."

Thank god.

"I'm not going to promise you a lifetime of happiness because that would be a lie."

I bite my lip.

"I'm not going to promise you any of the things a husband should promise his wife, but that isn't going to stop me from asking you to be mine. Huntress, will you marry me?"

He reaches into his pocket and produces a ring. A ring

he's made out of twisted together flowers similar to roses, but not quite. It has a green vine, thorns, and red petals.

I look into his eyes—eyes that say he cares about me way more than he should. He said he didn't love me. *Please, don't let him be lying about loving me. Please, let him hate me.*

"I hate you, too," I whisper back.

"Is that a yes?"

"Yes."

He grabs my hand and holds the ring over my ring finger. Then he hesitates as he realizes the thorns are going to cut into my skin as he puts it on.

"Do it," I say, not able to think of a better way to represent our relationship than with this ring. A ring of both thorns and petals—a ring of pain and beauty.

He slides the ring onto my fingers, producing little droplets of blood as it slides in place. Then he stands, takes me in his arms, and we kiss.

It's a kiss I never thought I'd experience—a kiss of a man who wants to marry me. A man I want to marry despite knowing the pain this will cause us both.

I feel the tears welling as his tongue pushes between my lips, but I hold them back. I won't cry in this moment. I won't allow any sadness to warp this memory.

I wrap my arms around his neck and pretend he just proposed to me in the most romantic way. It may not have been sweet, but it was honest, raw, and true. It made me fall for him even more.

Finally, he sets me down, releasing my lips. We smile at each other, before Langston takes my hand, and we start walking back to town. I make him stop at the same spot we did on the way up and grab more flowers to make him a ring too. Finally, we head back into town to go back to the church to get married.

Before we make it to the church, Langston stops at a

small shop in the middle of town. He turns me in the direction, and I smile.

"Give me just a minute," I say as he hands me some cash and I step into the small dress shop. When I was marrying Maxwell, I didn't care what I looked like, but now that I'm marrying Langston, I have this urge to get married in a white dress.

Most of the dresses in the small shop are beautiful vibrant patterns of the traditional Andean culture, to the point where I almost give up on finding a white dress. I decide to settle on any dress when I spot white lace fabric at the back of the store. The dress is simple—a low v-neck with thin straps and not much shape. It's perfect.

I pay for the dress and quickly change at the back of the store. I can't do much about my wet hair except scrunch it and hope it dries in beautiful waves instead of a frizz ball. Then I step outside, where Langston is waiting for me in a loose-fitting white long-sleeved shirt and dark jeans.

I drool just looking at him.

"Ready to be my wife?"

I blush, still not sure what being his wife means, but I'm excited to find out.

Together we walk back into the church, where surprisingly, Maxwell is still sitting.

The woman behind the piano starts playing, and the priest is once again at the far end of the aisle. *How did they know?*

We make it to the end when I realize that this won't be legal. "We didn't file for a marriage license."

"Shit," Langston curses, now realizing that we are going to need that.

Maxwell steps up, holding a piece of paper out to us. "Actually, I went back to the registrar when you took off with Langston assuming that you would be needing this and filed for you."

We both stare at him, completely confused why he's helping us.

"I didn't want to have to wait for you two to get your shit together. The sooner you're married, the sooner we can finish what we came here for," Maxwell says.

I suspect he's here to steal the treasure once we have it. But until then, he could be of some use to us.

Langston pockets the piece of paper, and then the priest begins. I get lost in Langston's eyes as the priest speaks, prompting Langston to lean in and whisper in my ear, "If you want to marry me, you have to say 'I do.'"

"I do," I say, biting my lip.

Then Langston holds out his hand, and I place the ring on his finger, drawing a trickle of blood as I push it on.

It all happens so fast that I'm not sure it's real. That is until Langston kisses me like he owns me. And for the first time, he actually does.

16

LANGSTON

I'M A FUCKING MARRIED MAN.

I thought I was before—to Phoenix. Turns out something got fucked up with our paperwork. Even though we lived that life, it wasn't true, at least not in the eyes of the law.

This isn't real, either.

And yet, when my mouth crashes down on her soft lips much harder than I've ever kissed her, I know that this is as real as it gets for me.

I dip her back in my arms, claiming her with every part of my body, slipping my tongue between her parted lips. My hand is already running down the front of her white lace dress that I plan on ripping from her body as soon as we don't have any eyes on us. I've spent my entire life sharing her—I'm done. I won't let any other man even get a glimpse of her ever again.

I start to pull away when she groans into my lips—her voice pulling me back to her.

How am I ever going to let her go?

I'm not.

She's mine.

119

My hand slides up her thigh, hiking her dress up her toned leg until I reach her ass.

"Get a room," a man's voice says.

I stop, realizing I'm taking things too far.

Our eyes open, and we stare at each other as my lips gently pull off hers. She pulls her bottom lip into her mouth as her cheeks pinken. I swear I see stars in her eyes.

Oh, baby, you have no idea what I'm about to do to you.

I pull her back up onto her feet, then take her hand. We need to get out of here now, before I take her into the church bathroom and fuck her in a dirty stall.

I turn, and then I see my biggest problem—Maxwell.

He's sitting in the second pew with a smug look on his face. I don't know why in the hell Liesel thinks we need to keep him alive. She thinks I was controlling before; she's about to find out just how controlling I can be.

"Stand up," I tell Maxwell.

He stands casually, putting his hands in his pockets like he's not worried for his life.

My jaw ticks. I hate that he thinks so little of me. He thinks that Liesel will save him.

I consider my options. I don't want to leave Liesel alone for a second, but I also don't want her to have Maxwell on her conscience.

I pull out some cash and hand it to Liesel. "There is a hotel two blocks over. Get us the most expensive room they have for the night."

She looks at me, wide-eyed. "What about him?"

"I'll take care of him."

She opens her mouth, I assume, to argue with me, to beg for me not to kill him, but she shuts it before rising on her tiptoes and kissing me with plenty of tongue. "Hurry," she whispers before she walks out of the church.

I stand frozen, watching her walk away. I can't stand to

see her go, even though we'll only be apart a few minutes. I still ache.

Maxwell frowns.

I grin.

Liesel trusted me. She let me decide what I do with Maxwell. I don't know when that changed, why she decided to trust me now with him, but she did.

"Shit," Maxwell mutters.

I stalk toward him—expecting him to run, to beg, to fight.

He does nothing.

What game is he playing?

I pull my gun out.

He keeps his hands in his pockets, surrendering to his fate.

"You going to kill me here, in the church? Isn't that like a double sin or something?"

"Why do you assume I'm going to kill you?"

"Because you are."

"Move," I say, nodding my gun toward the church's basement door behind the altar.

Maxwell walks with slow and steady steps, not like a man about to die. He walks like he isn't afraid of death.

He's like me—always knowing death will come sooner for him than it will for most people. It's one of the many reasons why my marriage to Liesel isn't real. It won't last, so what's the point?

We descend into the dark basement. This is the moment where I could torture Maxwell, get answers to my questions, ensure my family is safe and free the boy Corbin kidnapped. But Liesel is waiting for me in a hotel room, hopefully naked. My only goal is to secure him so I can spend the night with my wife. Tomorrow, I can deal with this bastard.

Every second I spend with Maxwell is a second I don't

get back with Liesel. I may have just married her, but tomorrow is never promised. Tomorrow she could hate me, divorce me, kill me.

I grab pull ties from my pocket while keeping the gun on Maxwell.

"Put your arms behind your back," I say.

Maxwell slowly removes his hands from his pocket and slips them behind his back.

I walk behind him, jerking him backward until his arms are around a pole. I tie his arms with the pull ties, and then I walk to the door.

"I knew you didn't have the balls to go against her," Maxwell snickers.

I fire.

He yelps and then stares at his thigh, where blood oozes out.

"Fucking bastard," he yells at me.

I smirk; there's his reaction. He is human, after all.

"I'll be back in the morning, to see if you survived the night." And then I walk the fuck away, to go find my wife.

LIESEL

I PACE back and forth in the hotel suite, still not believing what just happened. I have to stare down at the thorn-covered ring on my finger as the only proof I have that I just married Langston.

I. Married. Langston.

What the hell was I thinking?!

I shouldn't have married him. This will fuck everything up. It will distract us both from the task at hand. It will end up hurting him in the end.

And as much as I used to enjoy hurting Langston, I don't want to put him through the pain I know I'll end up causing.

So I pace—trying to find a way out of this that won't end in destroying Langston even more than I already have. He's my killer. My protector. He has a hard exterior capable of enduring any explosion, but inside he's sweet, kind, and warm.

Inside, he's a beautifully sensitive soul who cares about me more than he will ever say out loud. I pray that I haven't already ruined that soul. A soul that has to survive long enough for our kids to grow up with a father after I'm long gone from their lives.

I hear a keycard enter the door, and my feet stop. I gulp in huge amounts of oxygen as I wait for Langston to open the door.

The door opens like he's pushing the weight of the world away. He steps through and slams all outside forces out until it's just the two of us remaining. Everything else vanishes.

Langston enters alone, which doesn't surprise me. I want to ask what he did with Maxwell. *Did he kill him?*

It doesn't matter. I trust him.

Why?

I shouldn't.

He's a monster.

A killer.

But he's my killer. And now he's my husband. There are plenty of vows we couldn't speak to each other because we wouldn't keep them. But being loyal and trusting to my husband is something I plan on doing for as long as we are married.

My gut told me to keep Maxwell alive, but tonight, I'm trusting Langston's gut. If it told him to kill Maxwell, then so be it. We'll find Corbin and the kid he kidnapped with or without Maxwell.

Langston has a predatory gleam as he looks me up and down. I haven't changed out of my wedding dress, my hair is dried in long waves, and I've been itching to drink something from the minibar to calm my nerves but thought better of it. I want to be completely sober for whatever happens between us tonight.

I throw his look back, pinning him with my stare as I take in his thick muscles that his white linen shirt is clinging to.

The atmosphere changes now that Langston's in it. The air is warm, electric—a brewing storm.

He walks toward me; words have yet to be exchanged.

Tonight isn't about words. For the first time, I can fuck Langston without taking something from another woman. Phoenix gave him up. I still have to make a lot of things right between me and her. I owe her my life, and I plan on repaying, but I don't have to worry about hurting her with every kiss.

Langston grabs the back of my neck, and he pulls me into a wicked kiss. One that involves teeth, tongue, and swollen lips. One that radiates down my entire body setting me aflame. One that cements him in my soul, refusing to let go of this man ever again.

I have to be careful tonight. I have to guard his heart. I have to protect him.

"Why do you still want to kill me?" I ask him as his open mouth comes down hard on mine for another kiss.

They're the first words I've spoken to him since we got married in the church.

He stops his kiss, his lips pausing on my upper lip. He pulls back gently, giving me just enough room to breathe but not enough to not be exchanging oxygen with him. He thumbs the vein in my neck.

"Why do you still hate me?" he asks, answering my question with a question.

Because I can't love you, I can't keep you. All I'm going to do is hurt you. And I hate you for turning me into a killer. I already know my first kill is going to be the slaughter of your heart.

I nip his top lip.

He grabs my ass as I wrap my legs around his waist. His kisses turn soft, graceful like a choreographed dance as he carries me toward the bed.

Warning bells go off inside my head, reminding me that we shouldn't fuck in a bed like normal people. That level of intimacy, now that we are married, can only lead to heartbreak.

I grab his hair and yank hard, pulling his lips off mine.

He growls, not liking that I'm taking control or stopping his possessive kisses.

"Don't fuck me in the bed," I say.

He cocks his head, searching for the truth in my words, in my eyes. And then he grins deviously.

"I can still blow your mind whether I fuck you in a bed or against the window for everyone to see."

I shake my head as he kisses me tenderly. I know what kind of sex he's expecting. The kind that says more than I'm just a good fuck. The kind that has feelings and emotion behind it.

"I'm damaged, killer."

"I am too, huntress."

He tosses me back onto the bed. His body covers mine before I have a chance to escape. His hips press against mine until I feel his bulging erection pulsing against my sex.

He's mine.

I'm his.

But being his is as far as this can go.

I push against his chest, and my hips wiggle beneath his pelvis, only causing his hardness to rub against my clit through my clothes, inciting my brain with euphoria and making it harder for me to focus on getting my words out. But I have to—it's important.

"Don't make love to me," I whisper.

The corner of his lip tilts up as if to laugh. "I never make love, huntress. I fuck—hard. I control and sin with the darkest pleasures. I never make love."

I twist out of his grasp as I knee him in the crotch,

springing my escape. I run to the wall, pushing my back against it as Langston groans before standing up and stalking toward me.

"Promise you'll never love me," I beg.

He grabs my wrists and pins them behind my back. He twists me around until my front hits the wall. There's no way I can knee him now.

"I could never love you, huntress. You're a fucking liar. How could I ever love you?"

My eyes cut to his, and I know his words are a lie. I can see it in his amused expression. He can't promise that he won't love me.

"Promise me that a part of you will always hate me," I say, hoping that even if he ends up loving me, the hate will always remain.

He grabs the hem of my dress, his nails clawing up the back of my thigh as he raises it up. They creep around my cotton panties until he dips his fingers inside, pushing between my lips and trying to enter me.

I growl, not ready to let him have control of my body even though he already has control of more than I'm willing to admit, even to myself. My thighs squeeze shut, keeping his fingers locked between my folds.

"Promise," I demand.

His teeth clamp down on my earlobe until I squeal.

"I promise that a part of me will always hate you."

He releases my earlobe; I release his fingers.

Then I kick back against the wall, pushing him off me until I have control of my body once again. I run toward him, barreling my body into his open arms. I grab the hem of his shirt and rip the thin fabric in two right up the middle.

He pants hard, his abs contracting with each breath, taunting me with his fitness.

My nails scrape down his front, feeling every ripple on my way to his pants to rip them off his body.

He catches my wrist in my hands, denying my touch until he has what he wants first. His eyes drop to look at my dress, but he can't rip it until he lets go of my wrists.

He grins, as if he can read my mind.

"You want to play, huntress? Let's play."

With my wrists still in his fists, he dips his head down to the v of my dress. His teeth sink into the fabric, and then he pulls down—hard.

The fabric starts to fray, then rips in half as his teeth continue their assault on my dress. He continues downward until the dress is split in two, and my body is displayed in front of him in nothing but my white thong panties between us.

I yank my arms free before fleeing the bedroom. The bedroom is too personal, too sweet, too romantic. It's the opposite of who we are and what we can be.

Langston doesn't chase me. He walks slowly and deliberately after me, knowing that I want to get caught; I just don't want to fuck in the bedroom.

I glance around the living room, trying to come up with a way to have the upper hand when it comes to Langston. We've fucked before, and it was always incredible, but how long can that last? *How long can I give myself up to him before I lose myself? Before the raging panic returns, as will the nightmares of my past?*

Langston catches the fear in my eyes—so much fear mixed with want. It's a cataclysmic combination.

It only makes him move slower as I scan the room for a plan. I have nothing. All I can do is fight or surrender, and I'm not one to surrender.

Langston removes his shirt, baring all of his glorious

muscles to me before he puts his hands in the pockets of his pants and stands still, watching me.

I let my dress fall to the floor before putting my hands on my hips, mirroring his action.

We both breathe slowly; our eyes grazing each other's burning flesh.

"You're mine," Langston says in a deep, controlling voice.

"Then, come and get me."

I bite my bottom lip.

He moves.

I move.

One step.

Two steps.

And then we both attack. Both grapple for control of the other.

I grab his pants, needing them off his body, needing him as vulnerable as I feel.

I yank them down his legs as he grabs me once again in his arms and slams me back until I knock the lamp off the small table behind me.

I shove him hard, until his back crashes against the full-length mirror behind him. The glass shatters, no doubt some slicing into his back.

His eyes twinkle with arousal.

I reach between us, finding his cock beneath his boxers. I want to wrap my lips around him. I want to suck him so well that he'll never want another woman sucking his dick ever again.

He smirks and cups my chin. "You don't have to worry, huntress. I'm yours."

He once again reads my thoughts.

Then he slams me back toward the couch. We end up knocking the TV off the wall as we stomp by.

I keep squeezing his cock. He ravishes my mouth with his.

And then, all at once, he releases me until I fall back on the couch with him standing over me.

"Spread your legs."

I throw them closed, purposefully defying him and loving the thrill it brings me when he seethes and bosses me around.

He steps forward, kicking my ankles apart. "Spread. Your. Legs."

As I do, he steps between them, his hand moving over my thighs, spreading me wider. He kneels in front of me.

My heart is shuddering in my chest, feeling like a deer that's just been caught by a tiger.

Langston licks his lips like he's about to devour a feast. His eyes are a wicked shade of dark brown, swirling with the devious things he wants to do to my body.

And then he leans down, his fingers swiping my panties aside as his tongue licks down my slit.

I bite my lip to keep from screaming his name with one touch, but my hands can't stand to not touch him. I grab on his hair, pushing his head deeper between my folds.

He stops, his head popping up as he grabs my hands and places them on either side of the couch.

"If you touch me, I'll stop, and you don't want me to stop, baby."

I frown. "Why would you stop?"

"You don't get to control this."

I dig my fingers into the couch cushions, trying to give up a little control as Langston once again licks my clit with his tongue.

My eyes roll at the pleasure shooting through my body. My lips part, needing more oxygen. Needing to grab him, but needing Langston to continue more.

He takes his time relentlessly licking over my clit like an endless lollipop. It's torture, when what I really want is him to suck, twirl, and hum to bring my body to orgasm quickly, instead of this slow, torturous slog.

He has me so worked up that I can't control myself, and I grab his hair.

He stops, once again moving my hands to the couch before continuing.

"You decide when you come, huntress. Not me."

"What?" I breathe, confused because he's clearly the one deciding by going so slowly.

He smiles between my folds before his finger plunges into me. "When you trust me, you'll come."

"I trust you."

"You don't."

I frown, realizing I don't trust him because the fear is still there. The fear that a man I care about could possibly not be enough. I could revert to my nightmares having hold of me.

"Let go," he hums against my clit.

I do, exploding on his tongue as my orgasm pours out of my throat, and I call out his name.

I collapse against the couch, my head falling back as I catch my breath.

"My turn," I say, eyeing his crotch.

He stands and exhales, as if blowing out smoke. "I'm going to bed."

"What?" I snap up. He just gave me one hell of an orgasm, but it didn't do anything to quench my thirst for him.

He grins. "You're welcome to join me in bed."

I sigh and lean back, refusing to give in. No matter how much my body wants it, I can't give in.

"What's the problem? We've fucked in a bed before."

His eyes search mine.

"I'm afraid," I whisper.

"Me too, but I already promised not to love you. Isn't that enough?"

"No."

"Whether I fuck you in a bed, or against the wall, on the floor, in an alleyway, a car, the moon, it makes no difference."

"Then why do we have to fuck in a bed tonight?"

"Even though you'll never love me, you need to trust me. Trust that I won't ever let the fear win. The pain you're afraid of will never come as long as you're with me."

Truth—his words are the truth. At least as far as he knows.

I stand up until we are once again face to face.

"Okay."

With that, he takes my hand and leads me into the bedroom. He lays me back on the bed before hovering over me and kissing me so sweetly on my lips that it burns, already bringing on the pain. And he hasn't even fucked me yet.

"I've got you, huntress. I know you better than anyone. I've failed you more than anyone, but I've also protected you more than anyone." He kisses his way down my body, stopping to suck one of my puckered nipples before making his way down my stomach and over my C-section scar. He licks its length, before pulling my panties off my body.

He pushes his boxers off before reaching for a condom and gliding it on. We've fucked without a condom before, but I'm thankful he has one now. I've already failed as a mother; there is no reason to make me one again.

He carefully parts my legs as he settles himself between my legs until I can feel his hardness against the heat of my pussy.

"Trust me," he whispers.

I nod.

And then he sinks inside me in one pulverizing thrust,

the kind that has my head spinning with everything I've been missing, suddenly filling me and making me whole. I'm never going to be complete without him again.

"How have I gone so many years without you?" he growls, as always matching my thoughts.

"Miserably," I say.

He chuckles before his eyes return to his normal dark orbs. He lowers his mouth once again to kiss me.

I accept, and then he's rocking into my body. Taking his time. Protecting me from my demons. Caring about me when he shouldn't.

All the time he thrusts, one word hovers between us but is never spoken. Neither of us can deny it's there.

"Killer," I cry out as literal tears fill my eyes. *God, I'm going to cry when I come.* I don't care.

"Huntress," he returns my cry.

And then we fall over the devastating cliff together. One that will ruin us and leave us even more broken than before.

Tears roll down my cheeks as Langston holds me to his body, us both breathing frantically as we hold onto each other with enduring need. Like another force is already at work trying to pull us apart.

"You're mine," he whispers into my hair.

I nod.

His words are the truth.

I hate him.

I hate him. I hate him. I hate him!

Those words are a lie. I don't hate him.

I love him.

But I will never say the words out loud. I'll never allow myself to even think them again. The words are toxic and lead to nothing but pain.

I pull his arms tighter around my body, knowing that we are going to spend the rest of the night fucking—*no, making love*. Although, neither of us will use that word to describe this.

I can love him forever, but Langston can never know. I may be the devil, but the pain my loving him would cause is something I could never inflict on him. So I'll keep lying until our marriage eventually dissolves—that's the only way to not hurt him.

18

LANGSTON

I LEAVE Liesel snoring in bed. I don't want to leave her, but I should check on Maxwell. And there is no room service in this hotel, so I have to venture out for coffee and breakfast anyway—and new clothes since ours are ripped. I don't care if Maxwell lived or died last night; I just need to ensure that he's still in the basement of the church and didn't escape to go tell Corbin where we are. My need to protect Liesel and my kids trumps my ache to stay in bed with Liesel and watch her wake up in my arms.

The sun hasn't even risen yet as I stomp the couple blocks over to the church in nothing but my jeans. We barely slept last night, and I want to get back to Liesel as soon as I can. Hopefully, she won't wake up until I return.

My mind races with everything that happened last night. Every position we fucked in. Every sound she made each time she came. The way her thoughts spun between fear and something else that I couldn't figure out.

The fear is what fucked me up the most. She's afraid, terrified her demons will return with me like I'm sure they have with every other man she's been with. Afraid of giving

135

up control to me. Afraid I'll fall in love with her and hurt her. That's the one thing she'll never have to worry about—I won't be falling in love with Liesel Dunn.

When I get to the small church, I run down the stairs and find Maxwell right where I left him.

He groans and looks up at me.

"Did you have a good night?" I ask, leaning against the doorframe.

"Better than you did," he says.

I laugh. "So you spent the night fucking the most beautiful woman in the world?"

He shakes his head. "No, but I didn't spend the night fucking a woman I'm going to destroy." He looks at me with a snarl. "I'm going to kill you if you hurt her."

"Liesel isn't yours to worry about. But don't worry your pretty little head about her. I won't be hurting Liesel."

"Says the man who has threatened to kill her multiple times."

I grind my teeth to keep from exploding on this man. He's not worth it. It's true that I've threatened to kill her, but I won't anymore. She probably still deserves it, but I'm not as much of a monster as I used to be.

"I'll be back," I say, turning to go back up the stairs. I take my time in case he decides to beg—beg me to let him go, to give him something for the pain, give him food and water. He doesn't beg. He's tougher than he looks, but that won't save him in the end.

I stop by two local shops. One for clothes, the other for coffee and picarones before I head back to our hotel room. When I get to the bedroom, I find it empty. My heart skips as I see the light on under the bathroom door.

She's still here, I breathe out.

I knock my knuckles against the door. "Liesel, I have coffee and breakfast."

She doesn't answer back right away. There's a rattling sound coming from the bathroom that I can't quite make out.

"Liesel?" I ask again.

"One sec," she says back.

I relax and start laying out the breakfast in the small nook while I wait. A moment later, Liesel appears in a white hotel robe. Her cheeks are flush, her hair wet, and a soft, knowing smile on her lips. All my fears disappear as soon as I see her.

"Coffee?" I say, holding out a cup to her. Her eyes rake down my bare chest.

She takes it, and I pull her into a kiss before I sit her down on my lap instead of letting her sit in the chair opposite me. She doesn't argue.

We wordlessly touch and explore each other while we eat our Peruvian donuts and drink our coffees. There's a level of comfort with each other that shouldn't be there so fast. Even though we've known each other practically our whole lives, it shouldn't be this effortless to just sit with her.

My thumb brushes over the ring I made for her. "I'll get you a real ring soon."

I don't know why I say it. This isn't a real marriage. We don't even love each other. I wouldn't have proposed if it wasn't for the stupid treasure. But it's important to me that she has the ring of her dreams because now that we're married, she's truly mine. I'm not letting her go to any other man—not without a fight.

She frowns and turns to me. "This is a real ring."

Her words have a deeper meaning, almost as if she's saying this is a real marriage.

I nod, but it doesn't change the fact that I will be getting her a real ring soon enough. Before long, the flowers I made this ring out of are going to wilt and die. I need to get a real ring before that happens.

Liesel shudders in my arms.

"You okay?" I ask.

She nods. "Just cold. We should get dressed and go. We have a long day ahead of us." She climbs off my lap before I can answer.

"Okay," I say.

We both quickly get dressed—I in jeans and a T-shirt, her in cutoff shorts and a tank. Then we head back to the small cottage hand in hand to await our fates.

Whatever is inside the small house waiting for us doesn't matter because it brought me Liesel. It made her mine, forever. Whatever awaits us will be worth it.

19

LIESEL

THE DOOR OPENS to the small shack-like house. The old man with wrinkles around his brown eyes wears a stern expression as he welcomes us in wordlessly.

Langston reaches into his pocket to produce our marriage license. "Do you need this? We just got married yesterday, so I'm not sure if it will show up in the record system yet."

The man shakes his head. "I confirmed with the priest that you two are, in fact, married."

He turns to me. "I do need your blood, dear."

He pulls out a knife, and I automatically stick out my hand, offering this man to take whatever he needs from me. I'll do anything to protect my son.

Langston tenses next to me as the man pricks my finger.

I smile up at Langston, loving how protective he is over me. I didn't use to like it, but it sets my heart aflutter when he does it now that we're married.

"I'll be right back," the man says, carrying the knife with my blood on it away.

Langston hasn't let go of my hand as we stand in the small candlelit room, waiting.

"What happens next?" I ask Langston.

"I don't know. This is as far as Phoenix and I made it."

My stomach rolls when he says her name. I still can't believe how kind she is. Langston deserves a girl like her, not me.

"Don't," Langston says.

"Don't what?"

"Compare yourself to her. She has made plenty of mistakes with her life, just like you have. Don't forget she blackmailed me into marrying her."

"She also adopted the son of her enemy. She's a much better woman than I am."

Langston growls and squeezes my hand, obviously disagreeing with me.

"Have you heard from Beckett or Phoenix yet? Or the kids?"

"No, not hearing from them is a good thing. They will only contact us if there is a problem. It's safer this way."

I nod, knowing he's right. But after learning Atlas is alive and well, I want to know where he is every second of every day.

"Thank you for waiting, Liesel. If you will, please follow me now. Langston, if you will wait here," the man says.

I nod and start following the man out the back door, but Langston's grip on me tightens.

I lift his hand to mine and kiss it. "I'll be right back."

Slowly, his release on me loosens enough for me to pull my fingers out of his grasp. I feel every tingling nerve of anxious energy burst through him, and I want nothing more than to go back to our hotel room and spend the rest of the day getting lost under the covers to soothe him.

Instead, I do the right thing. I let go and follow the old

man out of the house. The sun is shining down on us through the trees as we walk down a small winding path to a clearing by a creek.

"Sit," he says, pointing to a small tree stump on the ground.

I sit while he walks over to a makeshift table that has a pot of tea and two cups. He pours each of us a cup and hands one to me before he sits on a log opposite me.

"I'm Diego, I knew your father well. I'm sorry he's gone."

"Nice to meet you, Diego. But you don't need to be sorry for my dead father. He was never around. I didn't know him."

"I'm sorry that your father didn't know how to be a father. You were better off without a father."

I disagree, but I don't say so.

"I bet you're wondering why your father sent you on this crazy quest. If he had so much money, why not just give it to you?"

I nod. "It does seem strange."

"He didn't want it to destroy you like it did him. He wanted to ensure you'd be strong enough to wield the kind of power that goes with the kind of money you would inherit."

"I don't know if I'm strong enough or not; I just want to ensure that my child doesn't grow up constantly facing danger and threats of people trying to steal from him. I just want him to be safe. I couldn't care less about the money."

"I think you have what it takes, Liesel. I can see it. All that's left is to prove it."

"And how do I do that?"

"There are three qualities your father wanted to ensure that you possess. Once you demonstrate them, you'll have all the clues you need to find the hidden treasure."

He sips his tea. I do the same and its warm, grassy tasting contents soothe the ache in my stomach.

"How do I prove these qualities?"

"Each of the locations you are sent to will give you a task. Completing the task on your way to the next location will be one step closer to proving your worthiness. We will be watching for proof, so no need to bring anything physical with you. But your next location is in Egypt."

"Egypt?"

"Yes, your father had friends who like to live where there are fewer people."

Like him.

He shows me the address of the next location, and once I've memorized it, he burns it in the fire crackling between us.

"What is the quality I have to show?"

"Betrayal."

I frown, not liking the sound of this. "Betrayal to who?"

"Your husband."

My heart thumps to a stop. "My father wanted me to get married just so I could betray him?"

He nods. "He wanted you to prove to yourself that even if you loved a man, you don't need him. That his love isn't enough."

I stand up as my blood boils. I'm beyond pissed. I want to go to my father's grave and pull him back to life just so I can kill him all over again. Everything I just went through was for nothing. I married Langston for nothing.

"What exactly do I have to do to betray him?"

"The only way that matters to Langston."

"Which is?"

"Be claimed by another man. Make Langston believe you're no longer his."

"How will you know if I betray him or not?"

"Trust me, we'll know."

"And if I choose not to betray him?"

"Then, you won't get the next clue, and you'll never find the treasure."

And my son will never be safe from greedy hunters.

I look down to the ground, knowing if there is a heaven and hell, my dad is most definitely in hell for what he's putting me through. *You couldn't be a father for the first twenty-plus years of my life, and now that you're dead, you decide to teach me some lessons?*

I look at Diego, defeated. "What do I do now?" *What if I love him?*

"You betray him. You get the treasure. You protect your child. That's what you do."

I squeeze my eyes shut, but the tears fall anyway. I don't know why Langston hates me. I don't know why he wants to kill me. But after I betray him—he's never going to forgive me.

LANGSTON

I'VE WORN down every inch of the dirt floor with my pacing in this one-room house while I wait for Liesel to return. Fear floods my head with horrible images of what could be happening to her.

Is she in pain? Is she suffering, and I'm not helping her? I could never forgive myself if so.

Finally, light streams into the house as the back door opens, and Liesel steps back into the room alone.

I run to her and wrap her possessively into my open arms. She doesn't speak. I assume she's going to act tough and try to pull away; instead, she sinks into my chest, letting me hold her as tight as I want.

I slow my breathing, trying to slow hers. Hers stays quick for several minutes before finally meeting my steady breath. Only then do I speak.

"What happened?" I ask.

"He just told me where the next location is."

My hand is nestled on the back of her neck behind her hair. I tilt her head up to look at me, and rage spreads inside me at what I see—puffy, red eyes.

"What happened?" I try again, this time as softly as I can manage, so I don't scare her with the fire I feel inside.

"We had tea, and he told me where we have to travel to next."

I can see the truth in her eyes—but she's also hiding something from me.

"What did you do to get that information?"

She takes a step out of my arms; she's not going to tell me. I could beat it out of her, threaten her, but it wouldn't work. There is no threat violent enough to get her to tell me —to trust me.

We haven't been married but a day, and she's already keeping things from me. The only thing I can do is earn her trust while keeping the burning disappointment that I'm not enough for her at bay.

Her long eyelashes flicker up at me—telling me to trust her. There's a reason she can't tell me, it's not by choice.

I sigh and run my hand through my hair.

"Let's go get Maxwell and then get out of here."

"You didn't kill him?"

I shake my head. "You didn't want me to, so I didn't."

"Thank you."

I grab her neck and pull her back into my arms, my lips kissing the top of her head. "I'll always do my best to do right by you. I promise."

I link our fingers together, and then I pull her out of this place of darkness that has caused her so much pain in such little time. I may not know what happened, but at least I can be the one to take her away.

I watch her closely, looking for any sign of injury as we walk back into town. I find none. Whatever he did to her was mental.

We walk back into the church. It feels surreal to be standing back in the place where we got married so soon.

Then I show her downstairs to where Maxwell is still tied up with a bullet wound in his thigh.

"You really didn't kill him," she says to herself in disbelief at the sight of Maxwell. She lets go of my hand and approaches him.

I'm not sure what she's going to do to him. What I didn't expect to see is her down on her knees next to him, ripping the bottom of her shirt to tie around his leg.

"I'm going to get you some water and pain killers, and you'll feel better soon," she says to him.

I frown, glaring down at him. I want to put a bullet between the bastard's eyes, but apparently, we're bringing him with us.

"Knife," Liesel says, holding her hand out to me in an annoying tone.

I pull out my knife from my boot and hand it to her. She starts working on the pull ties around his wrists.

"Are you annoyed with me?" I ask.

"No," she snaps back.

I roll my eyes. "So that's a yes."

She cuts the tie, and Maxwell falls forward, barely conscious.

"Did you really have to shoot him?"

"Yes, I had to ensure he stayed put and didn't run to Corbin."

"I think the tie was sufficient. You didn't need to shoot him." She slips her arm under his shoulder, while I do the same to his other arm and help him up.

We start walking him up the stairs. "He isn't a good man. He works for our enemy."

"He still didn't deserve to be shot."

She looks at him, and I swear there's a longing in her eyes when she looks at him, but I'm sure I'm just mistaking it for pity. She doesn't want Maxwell; she just doesn't want him dead. At least, not yet.

I call a cab, and then we all pile in and drive to the private airport. I'm on the phone making arrangements for our flight, while Liesel holds Maxwell in her lap, stroking the golden locks of his hair mindlessly.

Our pilot asks me where we are flying to. I snap to Liesel. "Where to?"

I don't expect her to answer, but she does. "Egypt. I'll give him the exact coordinates once we get to the airport."

I tell my pilot and then sit in silence for the rest of the drive, trying to understand what changed with Liesel between last night and right now.

We get to the airport, and I pull Maxwell out, carrying him sideways in my arms so Liesel won't have to touch him. He barely groans as I carry him toward the airplane.

Once inside, I lie him down on one of the couches at the back.

Liesel walks up beside me, carrying a first aid kit. "Do you want to do it or should I?'

I grab the kit out of her hands. I don't want her touching this guy.

I set the kit on the floor as I kneel next to him. I pop it open with a thump and begin searching for the items I'm going to need—gauze, tweezers, alcohol, bandages, stitches.

I go to work on his leg like he's a member of my team—not the enemy he is. I'm so focused on getting the job done quickly and cleanly that I don't notice Liesel holding his hand.

My eyes keep cutting to their joined hands. I want to rip her hands from his and suck every finger clean of the mere touch of him. I don't because I don't want to deepen our fight.

"I'm finished," I say, basically clearing my throat in a

grumbled, grumpy way to get Liesel to stop touching Maxwell.

She doesn't immediately let go of his hand. Instead, she digs through the first aid kit until she finds a bottle of pills. Popping the lid off, she pours a couple into her hand and then puts them in Maxwell's mouth.

"These will ease the pain and help you sleep," she says to him before holding up some water to his lips. He sips the water, barely conscious. The pills will knock him out. He won't feel any of the pain within minutes. It's too kind if you ask me.

Maxwell's eyes flutter closed, and only then does she let go of his hand.

"Why are you being so nice to him?" I ask.

She purses her lips, looking at Maxwell like she has a pull to him that even she herself doesn't understand. "I don't know, really. It just feels like the right thing to do."

I hate her answer, but I'm not going to fight with her about it. Maxwell will meet his demise soon enough. I start walking a couple of rows up and take a seat. I don't want to look or think about the bastard.

"What are we going to do about Corbin?" Liesel asks, sitting down next to me.

"I already have Enzo and Zeke looking for him."

She smiles. "You forgave them already?"

I growl.

She smirks and takes my hand in hers. The same hand that was just holding that monster's.

I remove my hand from her grasp and look out the window, annoyed with her already. This is why we would never work out.

"Don't—don't be like that. I don't care about Maxwell. I just think we should keep him alive and taken care of until we figure out how to use him to get to Corbin and save the child he's taken, that's all."

"I say we kill him. Corbin will come after us for revenge if he cares about the bastard at all."

She frowns. "I'd rather not piss Corbin off and risk our lives for nothing."

She's soft on Maxwell. She cares about him. And she's not a killer—that's my job.

"We can't keep him around forever. At some point, we have to take a stand."

"I know, and I think we should after we have the treasure."

I disagree with her, but there is no point arguing right now. All I did was stitch Maxwell up and keep him alive until we get to our next stop, where I'll once again have to tie him up and disable him while we go in search of the treasure. It's actually kinder to just kill him now.

"Look at me," Liesel says.

I take a deep breath and then turn and face her. I'm annoyed with her about how she's handling Maxwell. I'm frustrated that she doesn't trust me enough to tell me what she had to do to earn our next clue. But when I look into her big hazel eyes that hold the weight of the world—all of that vanishes. In her eyes, I see something I've never seen before staring back at me—an emotion that neither of us can describe with words.

She runs her tongue over her teeth as she climbs on top of my lap until she's straddling me in my chair.

"Kiss me," she says with a longing to her voice. She thinks I won't kiss her.

I don't hesitate—I grab the back of her neck and pull her down until her soft lips touch mine. I just had her last night, but that seems like a lifetime away. The bitterness that I felt melts away with a single kiss.

"I needed that," I say when she pulls back.

"I need more."

She reaches between the seats and flicks the lever that dips the seat back. Her eyes ignite with a burning desire as she rips her tank top off her body until two peaks are staring back at me.

My head darts behind me to where Maxwell is hopefully asleep and not looking at my topless wife.

"What are you doing?"

She grins as she undoes the button on my jeans. "Fucking you."

"You can't—Maxwell is three rows behind us. The pilots—"

"Are you my husband?"

"Yes…"

"Then fuck me. I don't care about anyone else on this plane. I need you."

Fuck me.

She doesn't wait for my answer. Her hand slips into my pants, taking complete control.

"Don't." I grip her wrist, stopping her.

"Why?" Her eyes sear, demanding this.

"I'm angry."

"So?"

"Maxwell could wake up and see you."

"He won't."

Her lips come down hard on mine, clinging to me like I'm the only thing in her world. "I need you."

"I'm yours," I concede.

Her next moves are frantic, crazed as she moves quickly to undo my pants. I match her frenzied state, unbuttoning her shorts off just as quickly.

I don't know what happened to her. I don't know what she did, what she gave up to get the next clue. I do know it was painful, though. And I will do anything to take away her pain.

She kicks her shorts off and angles me between her legs, straddling me again.

I move to reach for a condom in my pocket, but she's already sliding down on my cock. I don't give a damn if I get her pregnant. Kids I'm good with. And if she wants to have my babies, I'll give her as many as she wants. What's most important now is giving her all of myself without any barriers.

I thrust up as she slides her hips down over my cock—up and down like she's sprinting, trying to chase an orgasm that will escape her if she doesn't find it quickly. I don't know why she feels the need to rush, but I match her speed, not questioning her.

I tug her nipple into my mouth that's been bouncing at eye level as she grasps onto my hair, giving her more grip to fuck me harder.

"That's it, baby, get it all out. Fuck the pain away."

I grab her hips and lift her up and down, helping her move as quickly as her body demands her. Helping her to chase away her fears.

Harder.

Faster.

Deeper.

I thrust into her. I focus on giving her all the pleasure in the world—thrusting deeper into her cunt, lapping at her swollen nipples, pinching her sensitive clit. I don't even realize I'm on the edge of coming until she's exploding around my cock, and I shoot my cum inside her.

She breathes deeply as I grip her hips. Her head falls forward against my chest, and she inhales and exhales sharply.

I stroke her hair, letting her have a moment to feel and

breathe normally again. Her breathing does slow, but her eyes close as she falls asleep against my chest.

I shake my head as I lift her gently in my arms. I find a blanket a couple of rows up and drape it over us. Both of us are half-naked and my cum is sticking to her thighs, but none of that matters as she sleeps in my arms.

"What happened to you, baby?" I whisper into her hair, devastated by whatever it is she went through.

I close my eyes and tug her tighter to my body, kissing her hair. *How does she feel so perfect in my arms?*

"I lov—" I start and then stop myself. I run my hand through my hair, scolding myself for the almost slip.

It was just reflex. I don't love her. The only problem is I don't know if I'm lying to myself or finally admitting the truth.

21

LIESEL

I WAKE up as the plane lands; our rough landing jars me awake.

I blink several times, trying to remember where I am and what's happening. Then I breathe in Langston—his musky smell mixed with sweat and sex. I smile and snuggle into his chest.

"You're going to have to wake up and get dressed, baby."

Get dressed?

I take an assessment of my body and realize I'm naked except for the blanket covering me. Langston is naked, too, lying underneath me. And then I remember fucking him— how desperately and furiously I fucked him with everything in my body, unsure if it would be our last.

Betray him.

My heart begins to crumble just thinking about hurting Langston. I'm going to blast both of our hearts into a thousand pieces when I betray him. I've been cruel to Langston before but never when he was mine. I don't know how I'm going to go through with it.

Langston lifts me up so he can search my eyes. He knows

155

that something is up with me. He just thinks it's something I've already done, not something I'm going to do.

If he didn't already hate me, if we didn't have a history of lying to each other, if we loved each other, then maybe we could survive my betrayal, especially once he realizes that I only did it to get the treasure and protect Atlas.

But we don't love each other. We never will. Our marriage will end with my betrayal.

I force myself to smile and kiss Langston gently on the lips before I climb off his lap and find my clothes in a pile. I start putting my jean shorts and tank top back on, peering through the aisle back to a still sleeping Maxwell. His chest rises and falls, so I know he's still alive.

Langston gets dressed beside me as well.

"What's the plan?" I ask.

"It's dark, so we should head to a hotel to sleep for the night. Tomorrow we can go in search of the next clue."

I nod.

He gets up and walks to the back to wake Maxwell. He says something, and Maxwell pops up.

Langston gathers a few things in the back before walking back to me. He has a gun in his hand that he holds out to me. I take it and tuck it into the back of my shorts.

Langston nods his approval.

"Follow me, we have a car waiting."

I stand and follow him through the aisle and out of the plane. As I walk, I hear footsteps behind me.

"Are you feeling better, Max?" I ask, without turning my head.

"Good as new."

I smile.

Langston growls, irritated with me for talking to Maxwell. The easiest way to betray Langston is by fucking Maxwell. Maxwell is good looking enough. He's injured, and

Langston already thinks I have a thing for him. It would be easy to make him believe that. I'm just not sure I'm strong enough to do it.

My mind is spinning with how I could pull it off, how I could use Maxwell to hurt Langston as I follow Langston down the stairs. A flood of anxiety rattles through my chest, shaking me with every fucked up thought I have of kissing Maxwell, sucking his cock, letting him touch me—all so I can hurt Langston.

I try to think of all the reactions Langston could have. Him yelling, beating Maxwell until he's dead, or just wordlessly walking out and sending me the divorce papers later. I don't know which is worse.

"Wait," Maxwell says suddenly, before we step into our waiting SUV.

His words barely register in my whirling head.

Langston understands the single word, though. He pulls his gun out and starts firing before anyone fires at us.

I duck down and grab my gun, watching as bullets whizz by my head.

"Huntress!" I hear Langston shout. His voice is far away. I can't hear him. I don't see him.

I shoot in the direction the bullets are flowing from, but I can't make out who's shooting.

And then I see a bullet coming straight for me. I try to flatten myself out—it's all I can do in the fraction of a second I have to react before it hits me.

A body hits me instead—Maxwell.

He groans from the bullet lodging in his wrist as he pushes me out of the way.

Suddenly, the bullets stop.

Maxwell hovers over me, still trying to protect me.

I knew there was a reason to keep him alive. I just don't know why he saved me.

I look around the tarmac, but I don't see Langston.

A man appears, standing less than ten feet away from me in suit pants, a jacket, and an unbuttoned collar without a tie. His hair is slicked back with a few gray strands. He looks so similar to Waylon that I know who he is at once.

"Corbin Brown," I say as I stand.

Maxwell stands, too, cradling his bleeding wrist.

"What do you want?" I demand.

"I thought my letter made my demands clear."

My eyes scan the tarmac until I spot a body lying face-first on the ground.

No!

Corbin laughs, drawing my attention back to him. "Don't worry, your husband isn't dead. Just knocked out."

I don't react. I don't want Corbin to think he can use Langston to control me in any way. He already has a child he can use to do that. He doesn't need Langston.

"If you think I care about him, you haven't studied me very well. I only married him to get the treasure. I was about to marry Maxwell; Langston just ended up being closer."

Corbin's dark eyes glance from me to Langston, trying to decide if I'm lying or not.

"I don't have the treasure yet," I say.

"I know. I'm here to ensure you give it to me when you do."

I see Langston stirring out of the corner of my eye. A man stands over him with a gun pointed at his head.

I have to save him. *How?*

Maxwell is still standing to my left. He protected me from a stray bullet. He seems on our side. And as soon as Langston comes to, he'll try to fight. I have to protect him.

"I may not care about Langston, but you can't kill him. I have to remain married to him to complete the clues to get the treasure," I say, demanding that Corbin not harm Langston.

"I wasn't planning on killing him."

"Then, why are you here? You sent your minion to watch over us while we got the treasure. You kidnapped my child to ensure my cooperation. I'll give you the treasure; I just need more time."

Corbin's eyes run up and down my body, telling me exactly what he wants in addition to the treasure—me. I know exactly what I have to do to earn a little of Corbin's trust while destroying Langston's. Somehow, I have to use this opportunity to get the upper hand on Corbin.

I give him a wicked smile back as I run my tongue over my bottom lip slowly. Then I bite it as I sway my hips and start walking toward him. I rake my eyes over his body, pretending he's the hottest man I know.

When I reach him, he sucks in a breath, not expecting my reaction.

"I loved Waylon. It may have started off as him blackmailing me, but I fell for him. I always fall for the bad guys, the villains. I prefer the darkness to the light. I'm sure I could fall for you too." I pause, digging my nails into his chest. "If you want me, all you have to do is ask." *And tell me where you're keeping an innocent child.*

I wink as I let my nails dig down his chest, and then I strut toward his Bentley sedan behind him. I resist the undeniable urge to look at Langston. To see if he heard my words. To see if I've already broken him. To see if my cruel lies destroyed him.

22

LANGSTON

LIESEL WINKED AT CORBIN.

She flirted, used her body to seduce him. She touched him like she already knew him.

What is happening?

My mind buzzes, trying to remember everything that just happened. Every look she gave Corbin. Every unspoken exchange. Every word she muttered.

If you want me, all you have to do is ask.

She said it so flippantly. Like it meant nothing to her. Like she'd fuck him without thinking twice about it.

When she was just fucking me just hours earlier. When she's married to me. When she's *mine*.

I try to rack my brain for answers, but I only find more questions. Corbin didn't even ask to fuck her. He didn't threaten her. He didn't say he would force her. She just willingly offered her body to him. *Why?*

Has she been working with them all along? Did she lie to me? Was she really in love with Waylon? Does she actually want Corbin, not me?

None of her actions make sense.

And then another memory springs into my head like a bulldozer driving into my heart.

Kissing.

I was in the back of the van, barely conscious, but I saw Liesel kissing Corbin.

I open my eyes to darkness and find myself locked in a dungeon. Metal bars surround me, chains bind my wrists to the wall above my head, but the bars and chains are nothing compared to the darkness encapsulating my heart.

I shake my head, trying to shake off the memories that have to be lies.

Liesel cares about me, not Corbin. She wouldn't betray me like that. My memories must be wrong. She's in danger, same as me. She might be locked up in a dungeon nearby. Corbin could be torturing her, forcing himself on her. I have to break free. I have to go find her and save her.

I try to move my arms, but the chains holding my arms to the wall don't budge.

Fuck.

My feet are free, so I dig them into the ground, trying to gather some leverage to yank the chains off the wall. No amount of strength is going to get these chains to move.

I glance around the dark room for something I could use to pick the lock with, but the room is empty. I move my ass against the floor, trying to see if they left my wallet or phone. My pockets are empty. I move my foot around in my boot, but they don't find the knife I usually keep there.

I have nothing to use to break free.

I'm going to fail Liesel again.

I flail one more time, trying to pull the chains off the wall, but I have to force myself to stop no matter how hard it is for me to sit here and do nothing. If I do get an opportunity to get free, I'm going to need all of my strength to fight my way out of here, to protect Liesel.

A door opens, and light floods down into my dark little space.

I squint, hating the light. I prefer the darkness.

The door closes again as heavy footsteps creep down the stairs.

"Maxwell," I practically growl as he stops just outside the metal bars.

"It seems like our circumstances have changed. Now you're the one tied up, while I'm free to do as I please."

"Just shoot me and get it over with."

He chuckles. "Only an unhinged man would shoot a man while he's tied up. Especially when those men are on the same side."

"We aren't on the same side."

"Aren't we?" Maxwell grabs onto the top of the bars, his body slouching relaxedly as he waits for me to remember.

I glance up at one of his hands, wrapped in bandages.

He took a bullet for Liesel. He protected her.

I frown, completely confused about which side anyone is on anymore. But I do know that no matter whose side Maxwell is truly on, I owe him.

I sigh. "I owe you one for protecting her."

He smirks. "You're about to owe me twice."

He reaches for the lock and inserts a key, opening the cage. Then he walks to me and pops open the locks on each of my wrists until the chains fall off.

I rub my wrists as I stare, completely confused by Maxwell.

"What do you want?" I ask, knowing he's only doing this in exchange for something.

"I want you to go get the woman we both love. I want you to take her and get the treasure. I want you to save the kids. And I want you to destroy my brother."

"Brother?"

Maxwell nods. *Corbin is his brother. Waylon was his brother. He's a liar. Why should I trust him now?*

"You love Liesel?"

He nods. "I do. But unlike every other deranged man who has fallen for her, I know she will never be mine. The best I can do is protect her."

I don't correct him that I don't love Liesel. That I can't love her.

"You're here to help us?"

"Yes." He flings a gun at me.

I catch it with wide eyes. A man I've shot before just freed me and willingly gave me a gun. I don't know what his true motives are, but right now, it seems our goals are aligned.

"Where's he keeping Liesel?" I ask.

He frowns. "I'm not sure if Corbin is keeping her or if she's working with him willingly. She seems fascinated by him."

"Where is she?"

Maxwell scratches his head like he's not sure he wants to tell me. "Follow me."

I hold the gun in my hand as we jog up the stairs. Maxwell has his gun out, too, as we reach the top. "If anyone approaches, I'm going to pretend to knock you out. They still think I'm on their side."

I nod.

Then he opens the door, and we're standing in the hallway of a grand house. Without even taking a step out of the hallway, I can tell how big the house is. There are voices, but they are far off. The hallway is long, with dozens of doors.

"This way," Maxwell says, sneaking us down the hallway until we get to the end and it suddenly opens up into a grand room where the voices are coming from.

Liesel is standing in the center of the room with a drink

in her hand, while Corbin sits in a chair opposite her with his minions strewn about the room, sitting on various pieces of furniture, all looking up at Liesel like she's the one in charge.

Maxwell crouches down beneath a sofa; I slide over, doing the same as I watch Liesel through a crack between two sofas.

She licks her lips, her eyes darting around to every man in the room like she's taking her pick of the litter. I know Liesel uses sex as a weapon. I've witnessed it plenty of times. I just never thought she'd try it after she was mine.

She's not—it can't be true. Corbin is forcing her into this position.

Liesel struts over to Corbin, her eyes set on him. I know what she's going to do before she does it. I have to stop her.

"No," Maxwell whispers in a hushed command.

"I have to help her."

He shakes his head. "You do and we're all dead."

I know he's right. I count over thirty men in this room—all with guns. Maxwell is basically useless, and I'm good, but I can't take down thirty men while keeping Liesel from getting shot in the process. But I can't just sit here and watch this.

Maxwell looks at me and just shakes his head like he thinks I'm ridiculous. "You're an idiot."

Maybe I am—for falling for a girl who is followed by trouble like a hurricane leaving devastation everywhere. I know I'm about to once again risk my life to save her, but I'll do it gladly.

"What do you want in exchange?" Corbin asks, his eyes raking up and down her body like she's his.

"Nothing," she grins. "I'll fuck you and any other man in this room who wants me for free."

My heart breaks into a million pieces, each sharp edge

stabbing at my ribs and organs, killing me from the inside out.

But then Liesel's eyes catch mine. She sees me hiding—looks right at me as she breaks my heart and snickers.

My head falls back, and I glance over at Maxwell, who is just as stunned as I am. I'm not seeing things—Liesel just willingly offered up her body to any man in this room. She doesn't want anything in return.

Liesel Dunn is a liar.

She's never been on my side. She's always been on Waylon's and now Corbin's. She's the villain in my story. I should have killed her when I got the chance.

I couldn't then, and I sure as hell can't now.

Maxwell is right; I am an idiot.

For falling in love with a girl who was never mine. For still wanting to save her when she doesn't want to be saved. For still loving her even when she betrays me.

23

LIESEL

BETRAY HIM.

Do it—it's just sex. Something that's been taken from you so many times before. Fuck this man and whoever else he wants me to fuck to get the treasure, to protect my son, to end this war.

It will hurt Langston—but it will also save him. It's better this way. Make him hate me now so he won't get hurt worse later—so that there is no chance he'll fall in love with me.

I don't know what I was thinking, letting Langston propose to me like that. Getting married in a white dress with a handmade ring and vows. I should have just dragged his ass into the church and had a quick wedding like what I was going to do with Maxwell.

Instead, it was romantic and sweet and led to more. But we can never have more.

So I'll end it now.

My father was a cruel fucking man. If he wasn't dead already, I'd kill him myself for making me fall for a man only to hurt him in the worst possible way. Even if Langston figures out why I'm doing this—it's still unforgivable. It will still change everything between us.

I lazily look around at the men in the room. Corbin sits in his chair like it's a throne, while the other men salivate in my direction.

I have no problem fucking men, taking away their power with my pussy. It's when they try to take from me, that's when I have a problem. Sex is a weapon when you wield it correctly, and I'm an expert.

Before the last twenty-four hours, I would have had no problem fucking Corbin, making him believe I'm on his side, getting him to let his guard down in order for me to win. But now…

My eyes cut to the boy I used to love. The boy who is all grown up now and hiding behind the couch, staring at me like he's about to kill me.

I'm going to have to give the best performance of my life to pull this off. I have to betray Langston in order to get the next clue. If I fail, my son will forever be in danger. There will be no reason for Corbin to keep Langston or I alive. I have to succeed.

Before Langston came looking for me, I made a deal with Corbin. I'll do whatever he wants in exchange for getting to see the boy he's keeping hostage, a boy he thinks is my son.

I turn off my emotions as I throw back the rest of my drink—the alcohol burns all feeling in my throat as it sinks down into my stomach.

I'm saving Langston. I'm saving him.

That's the last I allow myself to think of Langston. My eyes focus in on my target—Corbin. He's sitting in a red velvet chair in a full suit. The only thing missing is his tie. He thinks the clothes make them look more powerful. And maybe he is powerful. He has loyal men, wealth, weapons. He thinks he has me.

He can fuck me, but I'll never be his. I already gave my heart away…

I straddle Corbin's lap. I hover over him, careful not to touch any part of him as I raise an eyebrow challenging him.

We doing this here, baby? In front of everyone?

His nostrils flare, taking the bait.

Why do I want to do it here in front of everyone? Because Langston is here. As much as it's going to kill him to watch me do it, I also feel safe and connected to him. I only have the strength to do this if he's here.

I grab his shirt, ripping the expensive buttons on his white Louis Vuitton shirt as I pop it open. I have to make the first move, and I just made it.

I'm the one in charge, not him.

I repeat that mantra over and over in my head as I roll his jacket and shirt off his arms. Corbin doesn't move to touch me. He thinks of himself as the king, and my job is to serve him. That makes my job easier. I'll be in complete control of everything.

I consider my next move carefully. I don't want to take off my shirt. I want to strip him first, so he knows I have all the power. But giving up part of myself, controlling his eyes with my body is more important. I'm the most confident person in the world and have absolutely no problem fucking him is what I need him to believe.

I need every man in this room to believe.

So I pull my tank top off like it's nothing, like I strip in front of dozens of men every day.

I can hear men clearing their throats. Others groan. Some look away, embarrassed. But most of their eyes are glued to my pointed nipples, inches away from Corbin's pupils.

But I'm not done yet. I stand up with nothing but tiny shorts that barely cover my ass. Turning around, I stick my ass out as I swoop it over Corbin's crotch and undo my button and zipper.

I force myself not to glance at Langston. I don't want the men in the room to know that he's hiding, but I feel his heated stare on me more than any man's in the room. His eyes are trying to demand that I'm his, trying to convince me to come back to him and stop this.

I can't.

Instead, I slide my shorts and underwear down my body.

There is a collective gasp in the room as I stand naked in front of a room full of men.

Corbin still hasn't touched me. He hasn't said anything either.

I turn back around, eyeing Corbin's crotch like I want to eat him for dessert.

He doesn't react. He just stares at me intently, not moving.

I trade his stare. I'll fuck him in his chair, just like I did to Langston on the plane.

"Such a brave woman to come into the lion's den and offer yourself up willingly," Corbin says.

I hold all my tension in my jaw, but I don't react. I don't let out any fear.

I can't help but think my father did this as punishment for all the pain I've caused.

He knew I was a terrible daughter, and I'd make a terrible mother, a terrible friend.

I think about Phoenix. I took the man she loved only to destroy him. I deserve to feel whatever pain Corbin is planning on sending my way.

"Kneel," he says, attempting to take control from me. But one thing I've learned from my time with Langston is that no one can take anything from me without my consent. He can boss me around, and I can follow. He can touch me without my permission, but until I give him something, he has nothing. He can touch my body all he wants; all I care about is my heart, and he won't be coming near that.

"With pleasure," I say, kneeling in front of him.

Corbin's eyes widen as he realizes just how far I'm willing to go.

"You really don't love your husband, do you?"

"I really don't, but I love to fuck." My eyes cut left, then make a slow circle around the men in the room before landing back on Corbin with a grin. "So who is going to give me the pleasure of fucking me first?"

I purposefully spread my knees, giving Corbin a direct view of my pussy.

He stops breathing.

I smirk.

"I want you to suck me and then every other cock in this room. Show us what a dirty slut you are," he says.

In my head, I roll my eyes. Men are such simple creatures; always with the dick sucking like that is somehow demeaning me. They would do anything I say for a simple blowjob.

I inch forward and grab onto Corbin's pants, yanking them down.

His cock springs free, already hard. It's thick and long, a decent looking cock, but my pussy doesn't get a drop wetter. When he fucks me, it's going to be dry and painful.

I lower my head to his cock, but before I touch my lips to his tip, I'm jerked back by my hair.

Langston.

He starts shooting.

Shit.

I thought he understood I didn't want him to save me.

Bullets start flying all around us. Then I see Maxwell. I

look at his wrist and remember that he protected me. He's on my side.

End this, I mouth to him.

He jumps over the couch and is by my side in an instant with his gun at my temple.

"Stop or she dies," Maxwell yells.

Langston stops, turning his head to stare at Maxwell. I know he's confused about whose side Maxwell is on, and I'm not going to help him.

"Drop the gun, Langston," Corbin says.

"You won't kill her; you can't kill her," Langston says, looking between Corbin and Maxwell.

"Not yet, we can't. But we can kill her child," Corbin says.

Langston smirks. "No, you can't. Because I have her child."

Corbin laughs. "So sure you have the correct child? And even if you do, you're willing to let an innocent child die? Even if she did love you, she'd never forgive you for letting a child die."

Langston sucks in a breath, and then his eyes fall to Maxwell, who nods, telling Langston to surrender. Langston still doesn't look at me.

Killer, put the gun down before you ruin everything.

Finally, Langston looks at me. For a second, I let a moment of truth fill my eyes.

Trust me.

His eyes glide side to side over mine, and I know he got the simple message, but he's searching for more—the reason I'm doing this.

His gun drops to the floor.

There's silence for a split second, then all of Corbin's men have Langston at gunpoint.

"You can stop pointing that thing at me, now," I say to Maxwell.

He doesn't lower his gun. He looks to Corbin for permission.

"Tell Maxwell to lower the gun or I won't fuck you. And I won't give you the treasure."

Corbin looks at me curiously. "There are almost thirty men in this room, all who work for me. If I want to fuck you, I'll fuck you. If I want the treasure, you'll give it to me. You have no power here. My brother will do as I say."

I shake my head. "You forget—I know who you are, Corbin. You're just like Waylon. You want me to want you willingly. You want me to offer myself up on a platter to you. Force me, and you're no more of a man than any other monster on the street. You don't have any power."

Corbin nods, and Maxwell lowers the gun. Apparently Corbin and Waylon's other brother didn't actually die—it's Maxwell.

A sick idea forms in my head. I want Corbin to trust me. If he does, he won't send his men to follow me when I go and get the treasure. I'll be able to finish the job on my own with Langston.

I could give up the whole ruse and fuck a random man on the street to betray Langston, but that only serves one purpose.

I walk up to Corbin, still completely naked. I wrap my arms around his neck and tug on his bottom lip roughly.

He growls.

And then, I whisper my filthy plan into his head. A cruel plan that is going to end Langston and set him free once and for all.

He'll hate me, forever.

He'll want to kill me and, this time, he might actually do it.

Most importantly, it will ensure I have the strength to finish off my own soul.

LIESEL DUNN IS A HUNTRESS.

She's always hunting, always searching.

And because of that, she's always been the enemy.

But now she's my wife.

I thought she was my friend. I thought that me taking care of her kid would have meant something to her. That our relationship, if not a real marriage, was at least sacred because I'm raising her son.

But everything I ever think when it comes to Liesel is a lie. *Why should this be any different?*

Who is she lying to, though?

Me? Probably.

Corbin? Definitely.

Herself? Absolutely.

Liesel is hiding huge secrets. She's hiding her very soul. I wish I knew if this wicked woman before me, playing her games, is the real Liesel or the one I had back in my bed a few hours before.

She's playing games with all of us. I don't see fear when I look into her eyes. I see a badass woman completely in control. A woman capable of burning this entire house to the ground, destroying us all.

I made a mistake trying to save her. She's more than capable of saving herself, and I lost my element of surprise. My skin is crawling from the way both Corbin and Liesel are looking at me right now—a failed protector.

Liesel is still standing naked in the center of a room filled with disgusting men. They devour her with their eyes, imagining filthy, vile things they want to do to her.

"We're going to play a little game," Corbin says, glaring at me.

I still have a dozen guns pointed at my head, so I don't move. I won't until I have a better plan, anyway.

"Langston, hold Liesel's arms behind her back," he continues.

Feeling any part of Liesel in my arms right now is going to heal my heart while simultaneously stir a storm that will wreck us. I don't think too hard about why he wants me to hold Liesel's arms behind her back, I just do.

A spark surges from her to me when I touch her first wrist. When I grab the second, I feel grounded again for the first time since I married her. My whole world came crashing down at me all at once at the single touch of her soft skin.

I hold her arms firmly behind her back, pulling her back to my front. No matter what happens here, she's mine.

Corbin grins at my reaction. "Since you already know I can't kill either of you until after you retrieve the treasure, I will have to resort to a different kind of threat for you, Langston. A game Liesel already agreed to play. You will hold her arms back so I can do whatever I want to her body. You will ensure that she obeys my commands. And if you let go, if you try and save her in any way, I will slice through her skin."

Jesus, it was bad enough when I had to watch her throw herself at him while hiding behind the couch. Now I have to hold her while he fucks her.

Maxwell gives me a look to say, *"See, I told you to stay put."*

I roll my eyes at him and then focus on how I'm going to survive this.

"We can still fight our way out of this," I whisper into Liesel's hair.

"I don't want to. I like sex. I like to fuck handsome, powerful men." Her words sound so strong, so sure.

"I don't believe you," I whisper back, trying to see if she's lying or not.

"That's why I wanted you to play, so you can see first hand how much you can't tame me. I don't care if you are my husband."

Corbin sits back in his chair as he grips his cock in his hand.

"Bring her here," he says.

I quickly scan to find every exit and count every man blocking each one.

"Husband, bring me forward so I can suck Corbin's cock," Liesel says seductively.

She wants him. I can feel her aching need pulsing through her. She doesn't have a good relationship with sex. Sometimes she controls it; other times, it controls her. She never thought she'd get married, and ours is a marriage of circumstance, not reality. I shouldn't fault her for wanting another man's cock—even that of the enemy.

Slowly, I push her forward until we are standing in front of Corbin.

"Lower," Liesel hums before licking her lips.

I can't watch, and yet I can't not watch.

I push her onto her knees, as I stand over her, holding

her arms back. At least I can keep her from touching him with her hands. At least I control one tiny part of this.

"I can't reach, hubby."

I growl as I push too hard, and her lips come crashing down on top of Corbin's cock.

This has to be a nightmare. This can't be happening.

I hear her gag on his cock as I pushed too far, but the sound quickly changes to moaning like she can't get enough.

I can't do this. I pull her off his cock, and yank her back.

Corbin's eyes shoot to me in an angry glare.

He snaps his fingers, and all his men descend on us. Arms yank Liesel from me and drag her toward Corbin while I'm held back.

Corbin twirls his knife around, and before I can blink, he slices it across her left breast.

"No!" I yell in complete shock.

She doesn't make a sound. She's strong, good with pain, but that had to hurt.

"Now, are you ready to behave?" Corbin asks me.

"Yes," I say through gritted teeth. I'll do anything to touch her again, to know that she's okay. Her back is currently to me as she stares at Corbin. I have to have her in my arms again.

The men release me, and I run to her, grabbing her cheeks and making her look up at me. All I see is hate.

She hates me.

All I do is hurt her.

I release her cheeks.

"Please resume holding her arms and hair while she sucks my cock," Corbin says.

I gather her hair in a ponytail with one hand, while the other grabs her wrists and holds them back. This is about protecting her, ensuring he doesn't spill any more of her blood.

I hold her head to his cock and watch as she sucks him, moaning with each head bob up and down. Over and over I watch, until my own eyes begin to water from this terrifying scene.

The room is quiet except for the sounds of her saliva and tongue licking over his length.

He grunts, and he's coming down her throat.

It's almost over.

I hear her swallow his cum, and I about lose it again. But I see drops of blood soaking the floor near my feet and I remember the price of me stopping this.

Finally, Liesel pulls her head back.

It's finished.

Corbin leans forward with a smile on his face like she just blew his world.

"You said I'm just like my brother. That I wanted you to come to me willingly, Liesel." He licks his lips. "In some ways, I'm like him, but there is something I enjoy more than a woman willingly submitting to me—revenge."

He snaps his fingers, and two men approach. Each takes one of her legs and lifts her up.

Shit.

I feel her body tense as I still grip her arms, now holding her torso up in the air. I feel a pull of her body to mine.

Corbin stands as the two men pull her legs apart.

I can't do this, but I don't know how to get us out of this. I have to find a way, watching her suck his cock was enough.

I don't know if the tense feeling I'm getting from her is real or if I'm imagining it. I don't know if she's begging me to save her or desperate for him to sink his cock inside her.

As Corbin tugs on her legs, she feels more like mine than his. *She's still mine.*

No matter what pain she puts me through.

No matter the agony.

No matter how many men she chooses over me, my heart is still hers. And hers still beats for me.

I don't know how to get her out of here safely, but I can take away her fear until then.

I find the spot on her neck—a pressure point used to put people to sleep, and I press my thumb against it. It takes a few minutes for it to work, and I don't know if I have that kind of time.

She squirms in my arms but tries to keep a composed face. At least, that's how my mind has morphed this situation.

"Trust me," I whisper.

I'm not sure she hears me. She continues to tense and then relaxes in my grip until she suddenly goes limp, falling into a heavy sleep.

I take a deep breath, finally able to breathe now that I've protected her consciousness from the pain. Now, to protect her body.

I'm going to have her words begging for him, her mouth willingly sucking him, in my head forever. And yet, I still fucking love her. Love is a strange thing I've yet to fully understand, but I do know that by the time we leave here, everyone in this room will know she's mine.

LIESEL

I'M DRENCHED in sweat as my body bounces up and down.

What's happening?

Where am I?

I open my eyes, feeling the weight of my body get tossed around in a leather seat. I'm in the backseat of a car, I realize when I see buildings flicker by out my window. I'm wearing my shorts and tank top again.

My eyes snap to the driver's seat, expecting to see Corbin, Maxwell, or any of their men.

"Langston?" I croak out, my throat dry and scratchy.

He doesn't turn around to look at me, but his shoulders tense, and I know he heard me speak.

I play through everything I remember.

Purposefully seducing Corbin.

Sucking his dick with Langston holding my arms. The connection I felt to Langston in that moment, making it easier for me to surrender myself to the cause.

And then Corbin approaching me, ready to tear me apart.

I remember feeling fear for the first time. But then I felt Langston holding onto me, and it didn't matter who was about to fuck me; all that mattered was my connection to him.

And then blackness.

I have no memory after that.

Did Corbin fuck me?

I look to Langston and around the car. There is no one else here in the car with us. I slowly sit up and look behind us, but I don't see anyone following us either.

Or did Langston burn all those motherfuckers to the ground?

The latter is more likely, but damn, do I feel sore and queasy. It doesn't matter either way. Sex with a man who isn't Langston is meaningless. Other men can do what they want to me, but I only belong to Langston.

"What happened?" I ask tentatively.

Once again, Langston doesn't answer. He doesn't turn around. His eyes don't so much as flicker in my direction. But the vein on the side of his neck bulges, and his grip on the steering wheel tightens as he makes a right turn.

Clearly, I won't be getting any answers from Langston, not that I deserve them. I destroyed a good thing he had going with Phoenix, and then I betrayed our marriage within the first forty-eight hours. I don't even think it's the betraying our marriage part that he's pissed about. The destroying our friendship and not trusting him part—that's what infuriates him.

I purse my lips and breathe out slowly.

I succeeded. I betrayed and hurt him. Now we can get the next clue. We can get one step closer to saving Atlas—that's what I have to focus on.

I assume Langston is driving us to the next location to get the next clue. I told Langston the exact address earlier, so I don't ask where we are going.

I just try to focus on my breathing and soothing the rattle in my belly, but I fail.

"Pull over," I say suddenly.

Langston doesn't listen, and I don't have time to argue with him.

I throw the door open just as the contents of my stomach come up.

"Jesus," Langston curses as he pulls the car to a stop.

I don't pay attention to what he's doing as acid expels from my stomach. I continue until I'm dry heaving. Even when there is nothing left in my stomach, my muscles continue to rid my body of all the shit I've been through.

"Here," Langston says. He's standing outside the car, just outside the spray of vomit on the ground.

I don't have the strength to look up. I barely have the strength to lift my hand to take whatever he is offering me.

A napkin.

I cling to it as I try to wipe my mouth.

Langston grumbles something I can't make out, and then he gently lifts my head up, takes the napkin from my hand and wipes my mouth. Then he lifts a bottle of water to my lips.

"Drink."

I do, but the second the water hits my stomach, I start heaving again.

Langston pulls my hair back as I dry heave this time. When I finish, he once again wipes my mouth but doesn't offer me water.

He looks at me curiously but doesn't speak.

When it looks like I've finally finished, he lifts my feet back into the car, then does my seatbelt before climbing back into the front seat to continue driving us.

My eyes water, not from the lack of food or pain in my stomach, but from the way Langston still took care of me even though he can't stand to talk or look at me.

He truly hates me, and this time, I won't be doing anything to change his mind on the matter.

A tear rolls down my cheek as I hug myself in the back seat. My life is truly cruel—to give me a man I could love and then rip him away from me so quickly.

Langston stops the car on the edge of town, parking it along the side of the round. He steps out and opens the door for me, offering his hand to help me out, but I can't take it. I have to start getting used to not depending on him.

I climb out on my own. Langston doesn't talk to me, look at me.

We walk in silence in the direction of the desert, down a path to a small house that sits on the furthest edge of town.

When we reach the house, Langston knocks, and we wait in silence until a middle-aged woman opens the door. Her hair is dark and long, and she wears a long tan dress. She looks between us and then motions for us to come inside.

It appears that Diego has told her to expect us because she doesn't ask who we are or why we are here.

"Sit," she commands as we enter a living area containing four chairs.

Langston and I both sit as the woman heads into her kitchen and returns with a cup of tea for each of us.

She doesn't speak, and I'm beginning to get used to the silence. After what I've done, no one will ever want to speak to me again. She looks back and forth between us, her eyes judging us.

"My name is Ramla. Please, drink your tea."

We both drink, hesitantly, like the tea is poisoned with a truth serum or worse. I brace myself for getting sick again, but the tea soothes the ache in my belly, and I'm able to keep it down. Not only am I able to keep it down, but the tea rejuvenates me and makes me feel more like myself.

Ramla continues to study us like she's looking for answers in the way we drink our tea.

"You did it," she says to me. It's not a question, it's a statement, but I nod my head in shame anyway, knowing she's referencing my betrayal of Langston.

Langston looks at me for the first time, frowning like he doesn't understand. I'm not going to tell him now; the damage is done. We need to get the clue and move on with our lives.

She looks to Langston. "I need you to come with me."

I frown, afraid of what is going to happen. I had to betray him, *what will he have to do to me?*

Hurt me?

Sell me?

Kill me?

There is no telling what my father's twisted game will require next. If we could bury the treasure forever with my death, then I'd kill myself. But it would only cause everyone to shift their focus to my child, thinking he can still find the money they desire.

Langston stands. He looks at me one last time, and then he follows the woman out of the room. I'm left behind to drink my tea and hope for forgiveness.

LANGSTON

HOW CAN I want to wring Liesel's neck at the same time I want to worship at her feet?

Liesel is hiding something from me, and I think I know what it is. I can't think about it too much, though. Right now, I need to focus on the task at hand. Whatever Liesel had to do before she left the house in Peru really tore her up. Something changed in her after that. I need to focus so that I'm prepared for what awaits me.

"Sit," Ramla says, pointing to a chair at her small dining room table.

I sit, and she brings me more tea.

I politely drink the stuff even though I don't like the taste. I have no idea what awaits me. No idea what task I'm going to have to do.

"Tell me everything you are feeling," she says.

I frown. I wasn't expecting that.

"Um…" I rub the back of my head. "I'm feeling confused, tired, angry, sad, frustrated." *Horny*—I don't say the last one.

She nods and gives me an encouraging smile as if I should say more.

But what should I say? I don't know what answer she's looking for or why this turned into a therapy session.

"I'm feeling hopeless, lonely, lost, heartbroken, miserable."

"Liesel hurt you."

I nod; she has no idea how much.

"Do you want to divorce her?" she asks.

"No," I say automatically. I want the opposite of a divorce. I want Liesel to be bound to me forever.

She doesn't react to my answer. I don't know if I gave the correct answer or the wrong one.

"Do you hate her?"

"Yes, but—" I cut myself off; I can't finish that sentence out loud.

She nods as if she understands.

"Do you forgive her?"

I blink at her, realization hitting me like a bus all at once. Liesel didn't do something to get a clue in Peru. She had to do something in order to earn this one. She had to hurt me, be unfaithful to me, break me, and she did.

"Yes." I forgive her. I already did before I even knew why she did it. That's why I was so frustrated with her—as much as I keep trying to hate her, I can't.

Ramla gives me a slow smile, before reaching into her pocket and sliding an envelope toward me on the table.

I put my hand on the envelope and slide it toward me.

"Be careful. There is a lot more darkness and danger coming your way. More tests to prove that your love can endure anything. Don't lose sight of what's important on the way to riches," she says.

"Thank you," I say as I tuck the envelope into my pocket before standing to return to Liesel.

She's still sitting in the same chair where I left her, sipping her tea like it's the only thing keeping her alive, which is probably true. I don't see any signs that she vomited again, so hopefully, she's starting to feel better.

She looks up at me with giant, expressive eyes screaming of her shame and fear.

Oh, my huntress, you have no idea how much I'm still yours. How I'll always be yours.

I reach down, and she flinches.

I deserve that after how I've treated her. She doesn't even realize that all I want to do is hold her hand.

I try again, this time making my intentions more clear as I take her hand.

"Did you get what we need?" she asks, looking behind me for Ramla.

"Yes," I say, and then I lead her out back to the car parked on the side of the street. I put her in the passenger seat next to me before hopping into the driver's seat and driving us away. I don't know where I'm heading, just that I need a safe place where we can talk.

Thankfully, Liesel doesn't talk, and she no longer seems sick—the pink has returned to her cheeks, and her eyes no longer look hollow as I drive.

I don't know how long I've been driving or why I stop, but it feels like the right place. There are no cars around, no people, just what looks to be some Egyptian ruins. Nothing big or grand like some of the more well-known places, but a few stones and an archway.

I climb out of the car and take Liesel's hand once again and lead her into the ruins.

"Sorry, maybe I should have taken you somewhere to get some food," I say, realizing my mistake.

She shakes her head. "I'm not hungry."

I open my mouth to say the words I'm desperate to say—*I love you.* But I snap my mouth shut again, knowing those words will just make everything worse. Instead, I say the next best thing.

"I forgive you, not that there is anything to forgive."

She gasps and blinks rapidly, trying to pull her hand free of mine. "You can't."

"I do. That's why I was so upset, not at you, at myself for wanting you no matter how much you hurt me."

She steps back.

I step into her space, my predatory stare boring into her. "But there was nothing to forgive, was there? You were told to hurt me. That was the only way we would get the next clue."

A tear slips from her eye as she nods. "Yes." She takes a deep breath. "I'm sorry."

I swipe the tear off her cheek. "You have nothing to be sorry for. You were given a task, and you did it. If the roles were reversed, I would have done the same thing."

"But I chose Corbin...I chose the worst thing I could think of to hurt you."

I shake my head. "You made the best out of a bad situation. Corbin trusts you now. He thinks you hate me, that you will do anything he asks just to ruin me."

"But I almost got us killed. I put you through so much pain. I made you watch while he fucked me."

"No!" my voice booms, halting her ramble.

I pull her into my arms, until our bodies are pressed together. "I didn't let Corbin fuck you. I couldn't. Maxwell couldn't either. We fought our way out of there."

"Maxwell helped you?"

"Turns out your instincts were right. I'm pretty sure Maxwell is a good guy."

"Where is he?"

"Hiding, Corbin won't forgive his brother easily. But you don't have to worry about Corbin hurting the child he has;

he thinks you are going to betray me to help him. You played your role well."

"Thank you for saving me. It wouldn't have mattered to me if he fucked me—I'm yours either way. But thank you," she says.

I tuck a strand of her hair behind her ear.

"Don't fucking thank me for claiming what's mine."

Then I tilt her head back and kiss her. We are standing in the middle of ancient ruins, in the middle of the desert, with no one around, and it feels like we are on top of the world. This kiss says *I'm sorry, you're forgiven,* and *I love you* more than any words ever could.

I don't know how I'm ever going to stop kissing her, but before I have to worry about that, I feel wetness hit my lips. Her tears have rolled down her cheeks and landed on both of our lips.

"What's wrong?" I ask.

"You were supposed to hate me."

I frown, not understanding.

"Promise me you hate me." She shakes me, demanding for me to hate her.

"I hate you," I lie. It's one of the most obvious lies I've ever said. I don't hate her. There is nothing that could make me hate her. *Nothing.*

LIESEL

I'm GOING to end up hurting Langston worse now. If he can't hate me for what I've done, then he's never going to hate me. In fact, there's a chance he loves me. That would be the thing that ends up killing him.

"Show me how much you hate me," I say.

"I hate you so much."

He grabs my thighs and lifts me up until my legs are around his waist as he kisses my lips again, stealing my breath, my pain, my fear. He consumes everything as his tongue bursts between my lips, commanding everything. My hands grip his head as he carries me toward a stone wall with hieroglyphics on the side.

"I hate you so much that I want to fuck you until your body realizes my cock is the only cock for you."

His eyes sear into mine, and I know he's serious, just not about the hate you part. He's saying one thing, but it's almost as if the way he says *hate* he means *love*.

My ass hits the top of the broken wall as he moves between my legs. I've never wanted or needed him more than I do right now. I need him to heal the chasm between us. I need to know that all the pain we endured and are going to endure is worth it.

His hand slides up my stomach underneath my shirt until he finds the point of a nipple. He squeezes, sending delicious currents through my body, familiar wetness spreading between my legs at the single touch. He knows my body better than I know it myself.

"I hate you more than I hate my father," he says.

I love you more than I hate my father.

I grab his shirt, lifting it off his body and throwing it down onto the sand. He frantically does the same with my tank top. He looks over my naked top half before he leans down and takes one of my nipples in his mouth, biting down hard enough to punish me for letting other men look at my body, touch my body.

"I hate you more than I hated Waylon," I say.

I love you more than I hated Waylon.

He growls at my words and kisses hungrily down my stomach as he undoes my shorts.

My hands find the front of his pants, and I start undoing them. I shove them down hard at the same time he rips my shorts from my body.

"I hate you more than I hate Corbin for touching you," he says.

I love you more than I hate Corbin for touching you.

And then he storms inside me in one long thrust, claiming every inch of my pussy. He doesn't stop to sheath himself with a condom. He doesn't stop to see if I'm ready. He just claims me.

"Killer!" I scream for the whole world to hear. A single word claims him as mine, just like he did me with his thrust.

In our world, getting married isn't enough. Loving someone isn't enough. The only way to keep someone is to do it over and over and over.

He fucks me like an animal. I claw at him like a raven ripping apart its food.

Every thrust inside me is deep, all the way to my cervix. He relentlessly pounds into me, and I want it all.

Every time I fuck Langston, I think it could be the last, and this time is no different. I desperately cling to every moment for as long as I can.

We fuck frantically like we are running out of time to be together. We are. We could have seconds, minutes, days, weeks, years. Our time together is ending, just as it's finally beginning.

I try to hold off my orgasm, not ready for this time to end, but I can't.

"Langston!" I yell as I come undone. I lose all of my senses as the universe shatters around me.

I don't know if Langston comes or not until I come back down to earth. I smile at his grin and feel his cum dripping down my thigh.

I shiver, and he cradles me in his arms as we sink to the sand, both of us still naked as we lean into each other's arms against the ancient stones.

"I have a question for you," I say.

"Same. You go first." Langston strokes my hair as I lean my head on his shoulder.

"Why did you want to kill me?"

He stiffens. "Atlas was really sick."

"What?" I interrupt him.

He frowns as his thumb strokes my face. "He *was* sick. He isn't anymore."

I exhale.

"His adoptive parents at the time contacted you for help. They didn't have the money or resources to get him help. And if he was going to die, they thought you might want to say goodbye."

I scrunch my nose, completely confused by why he would want to kill me. But I'm also heartbroken that Atlas was so ill.

"They said you refused them. You refused them money. You refused to help with treatment. You refused to see him."

I swallow the pain.

"I hated you for it, hated you for leaving your son to die." He pauses. "But looking at you now, I'm not sure how much I know is true."

I blink back tears. He hated me because he thought I would just let my son die. I regret asking my question now, but I need to know what his question is.

"What was your question?"

His thumb traces the outline of my collarbone. "Well, now, I have two. One is, did you know that Atlas was sick? And two…" I can hear the pain and frustration in his voice. "Are you pregnant now?"

I can understand why he's conflicted if he thinks I would abandon my son; he's not sure he wants me to be pregnant now. And yet, he's not sure any of it is true. If it's not true, he's hated me and wanted me dead this long all for nothing.

I don't need a test to tell me if I'm pregnant or not.

I know how I should answer about whether or not I knew Atlas was sick and in trouble.

One will be the truth. The other will be a lie. Both will hurt him.

2 8

LANGSTON

WAITING for her to answers seems like a millennium.

I suspect she might be pregnant, although, I don't know when she would have had time to take a pregnancy test, so it's really not a fair question. But she's been throwing up, and I've fucked her numerous times now without a condom or any other form of protection. It's a real possibility.

It's also a possibility that she just has food poisoning or hasn't eaten in a while and got motion sickness.

Still, she's constantly hiding things from me, and I want to know if I'm about to become a father again.

Liesel looks stunned sitting in my lap, like I just spilled a world of secrets onto her lap. That's why I'm not worried about hating her anymore. I will never hate her again. She didn't know about Atlas—that much I'm certain about.

"If you need me to take you to a pharmacy to get a pregnancy test, I can," I offer.

She shakes her head. "No, I already know."

My heart stops.

I love kids. This is the moment I become a father, again. And this time, I'll get to be there every step of the way.

197

She looks up at me like she knows she's about to break my heart. "I'm not pregnant."

My heart rattles around in my chest, not believing her words. But before I can call her out for lying, she continues.

"And I knew." She runs her hands through her hair in anguish. "I knew there was no way I could save him. No money in the world would be enough for his treatments. And me being in his life would only cause him to be hunted by my enemies, so I stayed away. I thought the kind thing to do was to let him die."

I stand to my feet, throwing her to the ground. "You were wrong. Atlas could've been saved. He's well now because I did what it took to save him. I found a treatment when there was none. I didn't give up on him."

Tears roll down her cheeks as my fury explodes at her.

How could she be so cruel? So heartless?

I'm steaming. I can't look at her. I march around the grounds, still naked, trying to reconcile everything I know about her.

Liesel is manipulative. She's controlling. And she has one mission in her life. She wouldn't let us give up on a child who wasn't even hers; there is no way she would have given up on Atlas, her own flesh and blood.

Something doesn't add up.

She wants me to hate her.

She's trying to force me into hating her.

It's not going to work, not this time.

I march back toward her, where she's crumpled into a naked, broken ball on the ground. Sand sticks to her skin. She looks hopeless and in pain.

Without a word, I scoop her back into my arms. She tries to fight me, tries to get me to let her go. I don't.

"What are you doing?"

"I'm putting you back in the car, driving you to a hotel

room where I'm going to clean you off, fuck some sense into you, and then hate you for the rest of my life!"

Her eyes narrow, looking up at me in complete confusion. She knows every time I've said the word hate, I mean the word love. It's a word I can never speak out loud, but it doesn't stop me from feeling it.

"I hate you, too," she whispers.

Her head falls against my chest, relenting to me. She's given up trying to protect me by getting me to hate her. I know a world of suffering awaits us, a pain like neither of us have ever felt before. But that's not going to stop me from loving her.

I kick up our clothes from the ground with my hand before carrying her back to the car. I pull my shirt down over her body and slip my jeans back on before I start driving us to the nearest hotel room I can find.

The hotel room isn't much, but we just need some place to clean up, fuck, and regroup. We can't stay here; it's not safe.

I carry her inside the room and examine it. It isn't much more than four walls, a bed, a toilet, and a hose hanging from the ceiling that can be used as a shower, but it will do.

I carry her straight to the shower, strip her shirt off, remove my pants, and then turn on the water. It's freezing cold, as I expected, but we are both in too much pain to feel it.

I claim her mouth with mine, once again possessing her.

"Your pain is mine; stop hiding it from me," I say, kissing her under the stream.

"It's not my pain I'm worried about."

"Stop suffering because you're afraid to hurt me. Stop lying and hurting me now to prevent future pain. I want the truth, not the lies."

She shakes her head. "You don't know what you're saying."

"I'm saying I'm yours as much as you are mine. I'm saying I'll hate you forever, and nothing you say can change that."

I kiss down her body, stopping at her stomach that looks swollen to me, but it's probably my imagination. She said she isn't pregnant.

But she lied—*about hurting Atlas or about being pregnant or both?*

Liesel grabs my arms, shaking me fiercely under the water. "Hate me! Hate me for real. I need it to be real." She bites down on my bottom lip, then slaps me. She's flailing desperately for me to truly hate her. She's purposefully trying to be cruel. But I see her clearly for the first time. I may not know all of her secrets, but I know her heart. Everything she's ever done is to protect her son.

She's the opposite of cruel. She is beauty and strength and all good things in the world. I'm the stupid idiot who ever thought differently of her. I just don't know why she's so desperate to add me to the list of people she wants to protect. *Why does she think me loving her is going to hurt me?*

I decide we aren't leaving this room until she gives me an answer.

My phone starts buzzing in my pocket.

Strange.

I don't answer. I need her. I need answers.

It eventually stops buzzing, only to start right back up again.

I groan and grab a nearby towel before picking up my phone. It's an unknown number; a tactic Beckett would use to contact me.

"Hello?" I answer as soon as I see the number.

"I fucked up," Beckett says.

"What happened? Are the kids...?" Safe? Alive? Dead? I

can't think any of the words out loud. But the mention of the kids has Liesel scrambling out of the shower, dripping wet with a towel and barreling toward me.

I put the phone on speaker so we can both hear.

"Phoenix took Rose and—" Beckett says.

"Okay? She's her mother. Just call her and tell her to come back to the compound where it's safe," I say.

"No, I mean she kidnapped her," Beckett says.

Liesel and I trade stares. "She's her mother. She can't kidnap her."

"Well, she did. She said she was just taking Rose downstairs to get ice cream. But they are both gone, and she left a note."

"What does the note say?"

"To give her the treasure or else she'll kill Rose," Beckett says.

I glance at Liesel, whose eyes are spinning. Yet again, she knows something she isn't telling me.

"Where is Atlas?" I ask.

"Maxwell took him. I tried to fight him off, but I wasn't strong enough."

"Fuck."

I throw the phone down in frustration, watching it shatter into a billion pieces.

Liesel sinks to the floor.

"They're all working together," Liesel says suddenly.

"What?"

She comes out of her daze and looks up at me. "They are all working together. Corbin, Maxwell, and Phoenix. Corbin played the bad guy, Maxwell our friend, and Phoenix the loving mother."

She stands up suddenly. "Did you ever figure out why you and Phoenix weren't legally married?"

I shake my head.

"I don't think she's my cousin. I don't think she's my blood. I think you weren't married because her last name isn't actually Dunn, it's Brown, same as Waylon. Same as Corbin. Same as Maxwell."

I rack my brain, but her theory makes sense.

"What else?" I ask, knowing she has more.

"The letter I got; it said something crazy. Something I didn't think was possible."

"What?" I beg frantically.

"You were at the hospital the day Atlas was born."

I nod. "I wish I had told you, and I could have held your hand when you went into surgery. I could have held you when you cried, but I was too angry with you. I was always furious with you because you never chose me."

She frowns. "I was pregnant with triplets."

My eyes widen.

"The day I gave birth to Atlas, I thought I lost the other two. That's what the nurses said, but the letter I got from Corbin said differently. He said I had three kids, and he'd have all three soon enough. I thought he was bluffing, but now I'm not so sure. You didn't take my kids and hide them away?"

I shake my head.

"You think all three survived?"

"Yes, and I think they have all three," she says in disbelief.

"Who are the three?"

"Maxwell has Atlas, who we both already know is mine. Corbin has Declan, according to his letter. Waylon's DNA proof all these years wasn't proof of Atlas, it was proof of Declan, I just didn't know it. And Phoenix has Rose."

"This doesn't make any sense, Rose is Phoenix's and mine," I say.

"Phoenix lied to you, Langston. She said she had your child, when really she had mine and wanted to keep you close to control us both. I think you've known for a long time. I suspected it when I got the letter, but I didn't want to hurt you. I didn't want to take away a biological kid from you because I know how that feels. But Atlas, Declan, and Rose are my kids. Somehow, they all survived."

I collapse on the bed in shock, as I come to so many realizations at once.

Finally, I lift my head and look at Liesel. "And now they have them all."

———

Thank you so much for reading Cruel Lies! Langston & Liesel's story continues in Dangerous Lies

My life is cruel, but so far, I've survived it. Survived the pain of giving up a child. But for how much longer...

One-click DANGEROUS LIES now >

"AMAZING! Talk about edge of your seat suspenseful, non-put-down-able, emotional and gut wrenching book. WOW, just WOW!" —Reviewer

JOIN ELLA's NEWSLETTER & NEVER MISS A SALE OR NEW RELEASE → ellamiles.com/freebooks

Haven't read **Enzo and Kai's story** yet?
I should have run away, found a new life, and started over.
Instead, I returned.
To find the man who sold me.
One-click Taken by Lies for FREE >

Haven't read **Zeke and Siren's story** yet?
She saved me. And now, seeing her about to be sold to the highest bidder, it's my turn to save her.
One-click Sinful Truth for FREE >

Love swag boxes & signed books?
SHOP MY STORE → store.ellamiles.com

Stolen by Truths #4

Possessed by Lies #5

Consumed by Truths #6

DIRTY SERIES:

Dirty Obsession

Dirty Addiction

Dirty Revenge

Dirty: The Complete Series

ALIGNED SERIES:

Aligned: Volume 1 (Free Series Starter)

Aligned: Volume 2

Aligned: Volume 3

Aligned: Volume 4

Aligned: The Complete Series Boxset

UNFORGIVABLE SERIES:

Heart of a Thief

Heart of a Liar

Heart of a Prick

Unforgivable: The Complete Series Boxset

MAYBE, DEFINITELY SERIES:

Maybe Yes

Maybe Never

Maybe Always

Definitely Yes

Definitely No

Definitely Forever

STANDALONES:

Pretend I'm Yours

Pretend We're Over

Finding Perfect

Savage Love

Too Much

Not Sorry

Hate Me or Love Me: An Enemies to Lovers Romance Collection

Ella Miles writes steamy romance, including everything from dark suspense romance that will leave you on the edge of your seat to contemporary romance that will leave you laughing out loud or crying. Most importantly, she wants you to feel everything her characters feel as you read.

Ella is currently living her own happily ever after near the Rocky Mountains with her high school sweetheart husband. Her heart is also taken by her goofy five year old black lab who is scared of everything, including her own shadow.

Ella is a USA Today Bestselling Author & Top 50 Best-selling Author.

Stalk Ella at:
www.ellamiles.com
ella@ellamiles.com